Laura Cadn

To Laura

Love. Nan & Pop.

Happy Xmas.

GRIMM'S FAIRY... TALES...

Also in the Piccolo Gift Book series

Aesop's Fables with illustrations by Arthur Rackham
Mother Goose Nursery Rhymes with illustrations by Arthur Rackham
The Water Babies by Charles Kingsley,
with illustrations by Mabel Lucie Attwell
The Baby's Opera and *The Baby's Bouquet*,
rhymes and music arranged and decorated by Walter Crane
The Happy Prince And Other Tales by Oscar Wilde,
with illustrations by Charles Robinson

GRIMM'S FAIRY TALES

PICTURED. BY.
MABEL. LUCIE
ATTWELL...

EDITED
BY
EDRIC
VREDENBURG

PICCOLO. PAN BOOKS

To
"BUP"
WHO . KNOWS . JUST .
WHERE . TO . FIND . A .
FAIRY . THESE . PICTURE
FAIRIES . ARE . DEDICATED

First published in Great Britain by Raphael Tuck & Sons Ltd
This edition published 1977 by Pan Books Ltd,
Cavaye Place, London SW10 9PG
© Lucie Attwell Ltd 1974
ISBN 0 330 24532 5
Printed and bound in Great Britain by
Cox & Wyman Ltd, London, Reading and Fakenham

CONTENTS

LIST OF COLOURED PLATES

THE BROTHERS GRIMM
AND
THEIR STORIES

TRULY we owe a world of gratitude to the Brothers Grimm.

Boys should take off their hats and girls should make curtseys to the memory of these two scholars who have added so greatly to the pleasure of our lives.

What would be the history of literature to-day without such tales as Little Snow-White, Tom Thumb and Little Red Cap? and surely the story of the ragged Cinderella is more universally known than even that of the great Napoleon. The adventures of the little maiden and her glass slipper must have been told hundreds upon thousands of times, while she has been the subject of plays and pantomimes, and her portrait has been painted by the greatest of artists.

Jacob Grimm was born on January 4, 1785, and his brother Wilhelm on February 24, 1786, both at Hanau.   Their lives were devoted to literature, and they were the leaders of a number of distinguished scholars who made a scientific study of the German language.   The Brothers Grimm held many high literary appointments, and produced numerous notable works, amongst them " Kinder- und Haus-Märchen."   These delightful stories, so full of vivid imagination, the Brothers Grimm collected in some instances from old MSS., but in most cases from the lips of the peasantry, for they had never been put into writing, but were, from generation to generation, handed down as Folk-lore.   And now, thanks to Jacob and Wilhelm Grimm, they will continue to be handed down in all civilised parts of the world as long as books are printed.

EDRIC VREDENBURG.

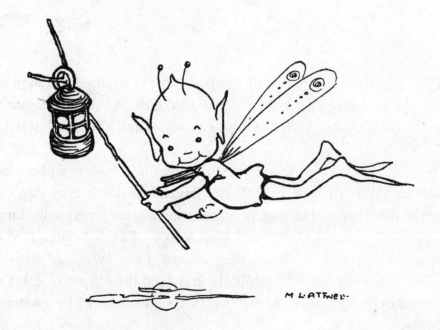

THE STEP-SISTERS AND THE DWARFS

LONG ago there lived a man who unhappily lost his wife, a very good one, and, at the same time, also a woman lost her husband. This man and woman each had a daughter who were acquainted one with the other.

One day these two girls went out walking together, and on their return to the woman's cottage she told the man's daughter that she would like to marry her father, and that if she did so his daughter should have milk to wash in, and wine to drink, but that her own child should only have water to wash in, and water to drink.

The man's daughter, when she went home, repeated to her father what the woman had been saying, upon which he remarked, "Marriage is a serious matter, it may turn out well, or it may be unfortunate," and not being able to come to a decision as to how to act for the best, he took off one of his boots which had a big hole in the sole, and handing it to his daughter told her to carry it into the passage and hang it on to a nail, then to pour water into it, and should the water remain in the boot he would marry again, but if it ran out at the hole he would not do so.

The girl took the boot as her father desired, and the water closed up the hole so that it did not run through. When she went to her father saying what had happened, he came himself to make sure such was the case, but finding it so, he visited the widow and wooed her, and shortly afterwards the wedding took place.

When the girls came to open their doors the day after the marriage, outside that of the man's daughter stood milk and wine, but at the woman's daughter's door stood water only. The morning after that, however, water only was found outside the doors of both the girls, and on the morning following, for the woman's daughter was placed wine to drink and milk to wash in, and for the man's daughter water only, and this happened always afterwards, for the woman was cruelly unkind to her step-daughter, and did all she could to make her unhappy, being jealous because her own daughter was ugly and disagreeable, while the other was possessed of great beauty both of body and mind.

On a winter's day when the earth was white with snow, and everything was like a stone, it was freezing so hard, the woman called the maiden to her, and said, "I have a great longing to eat strawberries, take this basket into the wood, and gather me some, do not return until it is quite full." Then she gave the man's daughter a dress of paper, which she had made on purpose, and told her to put it on.

But the man's daughter said:

"Strawberries do not grow in the winter, everything is frozen hard, and the ground is covered with snow; how can I fill this basket? And why should I put on a paper dress? the bitter wind will blow through it, and in the wood the thorns will tear it to shreds."

"Do you dare to gainsay me?" cried the step-mother. "Go directly, and don't let me see you again until the basket is filled," and giving her a dry piece of bread, saying it would be enough to last her the day, she thought to herself, "she will surely freeze and die of cold and hunger, and I shall never again set eyes on her."

Then the maiden did as she was ordered, she put on the paper dress, and, taking the basket, set forth. Everywhere was a thick coating of snow, no sign of anything green was visible, neither on the hill nor in the dale.

On coming into the wood the girl saw a little hut, and out of it three dwarfs were peeping.

After bidding them good-morning, she tapped gently at their door. They invited her in; entering she sat down on a stool near the fire, so that she could get warm and eat her breakfast.

The dwarfs seeing her piece of bread, demanded "Give some to us."

"With pleasure," replied the girl dividing it into two portions and giving them one.

Then they enquired, "How will such a flimsy dress do for you in the wintry woods?"

"Alas! I cannot say," she answered. "I must pluck a basketful of strawberries, without them I may not go back to my home."

Having now finished her piece of bread, the dwarfs handed her

a broom, telling her to sweep away the snow from their back door.

When she had gone out to do this, they consulted together saying, "She shared her bread with us, and is so amiable and good; what shall we give her?"

"I will make her daily become more beautiful," said the first.

"Golden coins shall fall from her lips whenever she utters a word," said the second.

"She shall be the bride of a king," said the third.

Meanwhile the poor girl had been sweeping away the snow at the back of the hut, as the dwarfs had told her to do. And what did she find, do you think? Why, strawberries, deliciously ripe, and looking very tempting amongst the snow.

Greatly delighted she filled her basket as quickly as she could. Then shaking hands with the dwarfs, with many thanks, she ran off home, anxious to please her step-mother by showing her what she had so strongly desired to have.

As soon as she went into the cottage, and said "Good-evening," from her lips dropped a golden coin, and while she was recounting what had occurred in the wood, at every word she uttered a golden coin fell, until they lay all over the floor.

"Just see how wasteful she is, throwing away gold like that," exclaimed the step-sister, but in truth she was jealous, and nothing would do but that she, too, should go to the wood in search of strawberries.

"No! indeed, dear child, you would freeze," her mother told her, but the girl insisted upon going, until at last her mother consented. Then she made her a cosy fur dress, and put it upon her, and cake and bread and butter she provided for her to take.

When the girl set out she went straight to the dwarfs' hut. She saw them all peeping out, but did not wish them good-day. She went clumsily into their room, and seating herself on the stool by their fire, took out her cake and began to eat.

"Give some to us," cried the three dwarfs!

"How can you have any when there is not sufficient for me?" she answered.

As soon as she had finished eating, the dwarfs showed her a broom, saying, "Take it, and sweep away the snow from our back door."

"Do it yourselves. I'm not here to wait upon you," she replied. Then after staying awhile, as they did not appear to intend bestowing any gift upon her she left the hut.

As soon as she had gone the three dwarfs held a consultation as to what should be done to her.

"She shall grow uglier day by day," announced the first.

"Whenever she speaks a toad shall come from her mouth," was the decision of the second.

"She shall come to a miserable end," said the third.

In the meantime the girl was hunting around for strawberries, but not discovering any, in a very bad temper she went home.

No sooner did she open her mouth to tell her mother what had happened, than a toad fell to the ground, and at each word she uttered another fell, so that every one was filled with horror.

All this put the step-mother into a furious passion, and seeing her husband's daughter's beauty day by day increasing, she constantly meditated how she could do her harm.

One day she put upon the girl's arm some yarn, and, giving her a hatchet, ordered her to go to the river, which was still frozen, and after making a hole in the ice, to rinse the yarn.

Obediently the maiden went to the riverside, but while she was breaking the ice there drove past a handsome carriage. In it sat the King, who commanded the coachman to stop, while he thus addressed the girl.

" Who are you, my child, and what are you doing ? "

" I am a poor girl, rinsing yarn," was the reply. The King felt pity for her, and perceiving how beautiful she was, he asked her if she would go away with him.

To this she willingly consented, for she could not but be glad to depart from her cruel mother and sister who loved her not at all.

So then the King took her into the carriage and went on his way, and on arriving at his palace, with great splendour their marriage took place.

A year passed by, and at the end of that time the young Queen had a son. Upon which, for they had heard of her great good fortune, the step-mother and her daughter came to visit her at the palace.

As the King was out, and the Queen alone, the wicked woman lifted her by the head, while the daughter took her by the feet, and together they carried the poor young Queen from her bed, and, unfastening the window, cast her through it into the river that flowed past the palace walls.

Instead of the Queen, the step-mother placed her ugly daughter in the bed, covering her up so that she could not be seen at all.

Soon after this the King came back to the palace, and desired to speak with the Queen, but the step-mother requested him to refrain from doing so, saying that his wife required rest.

Not imagining anything wrong, the King went to his own apartments, but coming the next morning to the supposed Queen, as she replied to his questions, to his horror, instead of, as usual, golden coins falling from her lips, at every word she uttered a toad appeared.

Full of terror he demanded the reason of this, but the old woman, who was near by, told him it was nothing serious, and that it would not last long.

That night, at the midnight hour, the scullion perceived a duck swimming along in the gutter. The duck spoke,

"King, what are you doing now, sleeping or waking?"
Receiving no reply, she went on. "My guests, what are they
doing?" "They are fast asleep," answered the scullion.

"My child, what is he doing?" questioned the duck.

"He is asleep in his cradle," replied the scullion.

Then the Queen took on her own shape, and, going upstairs,
she nursed her baby, arranged his little bed, tucked him up, and
then in the form of a duck, went swimming back through the gutter.

Two nights the same thing occurred, but upon the third she
ordered the scullion to tell the King to bring his sword and wave it
over her thrice. This was done, and as the King flourished his
sword for the third time, the duck disappeared, and there was his
own rightful Queen, alive and beautiful.

The King rejoiced greatly, but he hid the Queen away until
the Sunday upon which his little son was to be christened.

When the ceremony had taken place he enquired,

"What fate does anyone deserve, who takes another out of bed, and throws her into the river?"

To this the old woman replied:

"She deserves nothing short of being placed in a cask stuck all around inside with nails, and rolled adown hill into the water."

"You have pronounced your own fate," announced the King, and he ordered the cask to be brought.

Into it were put the step-mother and her daughter, the cover was nailed on, and then the cask with the wicked creatures it contained, rolled down right into the river and was never seen again.

HANSEL AND GRETHEL

ONCE upon a time there dwelt near a large wood a poor woodcutter, with his wife and two children by his former marriage, a boy called Hansel, and a girl named Grethel. He had little enough to break or bite; and once, when there was a great famine in the land, he could hardly procure even his daily bread; and as he lay thinking in his bed one night, he sighed, and said to his wife, " What will become of us ? How can we feed our children, when we have no more than we can eat ourselves ? "

" Know then, my husband," answered she, " we will lead them away, quite early in the morning, into the thickest part of the wood, and there make them a fire, and give them each a little piece of bread; then we will go to our work, and leave them alone, so that they will not find the way home again, and we shall be freed from them." "No, wife," replied he, "that I can never do; how can you bring your heart to leave my children all alone in the wood; for the wild beasts will soon come and tear them to pieces?"

"Oh, you simpleton!" said she, "then we must all four die of hunger; you had better plane the coffins for us." But she left him no peace till he consented, saying, "Ah, but I shall miss the poor children."

The two children, however, had not gone to sleep for very hunger, and so they overheard what the stepmother said to their father. Grethel wept bitterly, and said to Hansel, "What will become of us?" "Be quiet, Grethel," said he; "do not cry—I will soon help you." And as soon as their parents had gone to sleep, he got up, put on his coat, and, unbarring the back door, went out. The moon shone brightly, and the white pebbles which lay before the door seemed like silver pieces, they glittered so brightly. Hansel stooped down, and put as many into his pocket as it would hold; and then going back he said to Grethel, "Be of good cheer, dear sister, and sleep in peace; God will not forsake us." And so saying, he went to bed again.

The next morning, before the sun arose, the wife went and awoke the two children. "Get up, you lazy brats; we are going into the forest to chop wood." Then she gave them each a piece of bread, saying, "There is something for your dinner; do not eat it before the time, for you will get nothing else." Grethel took the bread in her apron, for Hansel's pocket was full of pebbles; and so they all set out upon their way. When they had gone a little distance, Hansel stood still, and peeped back at the house; and this he repeated several times, till his father said, "Hansel, what are you looking at, and why do you lag behind? Take care, and remember your legs."

"Ah, father," said Hansel, "I am looking at my white cat sitting upon the roof of the house, and trying to say good-bye." "You simpleton!" said the wife, "that is not a cat; it is only the sun shining on the white chimney." But in reality Hansel was not looking at a cat; but every time he stopped, he dropped a pebble out of his pocket upon the path.

When they came to the middle of the forest, the father told the children to collect sticks, and he would make them a fire, so that they should not be cold. So Hansel and Grethel gathered together quite a little mount of twigs. Then they set fire to them; and as the flame burnt up high, the wife said, "Now, you children, lie down near the fire, and rest yourselves, whilst we go into the forest and chop more wood; when we are ready we will come and call you."

Hansel and Grethel sat down by the fire, and when it was noon, each ate the piece of bread; and because they could hear the blows of an axe they thought their father was near; but it was not an axe, but a branch which he had bound to an old tree, so as to be blown to and fro by the wind. They waited so long, that at last their eyes closed from weariness, and they fell fast asleep. When they awoke, it was quite dark, and Grethel began to cry, " How shall we get out of the wood ? " But Hansel tried to comfort her by saying, " Wait a little while till the moon rises, and then we will quickly find the way." The moon shone forth, and Hansel taking his sister's hand, followed the pebbles, which glittered like new-coined

M L A

silver pieces, and showed them the way. All night long they walked on, and as day broke they came to their father's house. They knocked at the door, and when the wife opened it, and saw Hansel and Grethel, she exclaimed, "You wicked children! why did you sleep so long in the wood? We thought you were never coming home again." But their father was extremely glad, for it had grieved his heart to leave them all alone.

Not long afterwards there was again great scarcity in every corner of the land; and one night the children overheard their mother saying to their father, "Everything is once more consumed; we have only half a loaf left, and then the song is ended: the children must be sent away. We will take them deeper into the wood, so that they may not find the way out again; it is the only means of escape for us."

But her husband felt heavy at heart, and thought, "It were better to share the last crust with the children." His wife, however, would listen to nothing that he said, and scolded and reproached him without end.

He who says A must say B too; and he who consents the first time must also the second.

The children, though, had heard the conversation as they lay awake, and as soon as their parents went to sleep Hansel got up, intending to pick up some pebbles as before; but the wife had locked the door, so that he could not get out. Nevertheless he comforted Grethel, saying, "Do not weep; sleep in quiet; the good God will not forsake us."

Early in the morning

the stepmother came and pulled them out of bed, and gave them each a slice of bread, which was still smaller than the former piece. On the way, Hansel broke his in his pocket, and, stooping every now and then, dropped a crumb upon the path. " Hansel, why do you stop and look about?" said the father, " keep in the path." " I am looking at my little dove," answered Hansel, " nodding a good-bye to me." " Simpleton !" said the wife, " that is no dove, but only the sun shining on the chimney." But Hansel kept still dropping crumbs as he went along.

The mother led the children deep into the wood, where they had never been before, and there making a gigantic fire, she said to them, " Sit down here and rest, and when you feel tired you can sleep for a little while. We are going into the forest to hew wood, and in the evening, when we are ready, we will come and fetch you again."

When noon came, Grethel shared her bread with Hansel, who had strewn his on the path. Then they went to sleep ; but the evening arrived and no one came to visit the poor children, and in the dark night they awoke, and Hansel comforted his sister by saying, " Only wait, Grethel, till the moon comes out, then we shall see the crumbs of bread which I have dropped, and they will show us the way home." The moon shone and they got up, but they could not see any crumbs, for the thousands of birds which had been flying about in the woods and fields had picked them all up. Hansel kept saying to Grethel, " We will soon find the way ; " but they did not, and they walked the whole night long and the next day, but still they did not come out of the wood ; and they got so hungry, for they had nothing to eat but the berries which they found upon the bushes. Soon they were so tired that they could not drag themselves along, so they lay down under a tree and again they went to sleep.

It was now the third morning since they had left their father's house, and they still walked on ; but they only found themselves deeper, and deeper, and deeper in the wood, and Hansel felt that if help did not come very soon they must die of hunger. As soon as it was noon they saw a beautiful snow-white bird sitting upon a bough, which sang so sweetly that they stood still and listened to it. It soon left off, and spreading its wings flew away; they followed it until it arrived at a cottage, upon the roof of which it perched; and when they went close up to the cottage they saw that it was made of bread and cakes, and the window-panes were of clear sugar.

"We will go in here," said Hansel, "and have a glorious feast. I will eat a piece of the roof, and you can eat the window. Will they not be sweet?" So Hansel reached up and broke a piece off the roof, in order to see how it tasted; while Grethel stepped up to the window and began to bite it. Then a sweet voice called out in the room, "Tip-tap, tip-tap, who knocks at my door?" and the children answered, "The wind, the wind, the child of heaven;" and they went on eating without interruption. Hansel thought the roof tasted very nice, and so he tore off a great piece; while Grethel broke

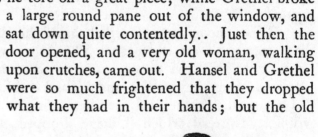

a large round pane out of the window, and sat down quite contentedly.. Just then the door opened, and a very old woman, walking upon crutches, came out. Hansel and Grethel were so much frightened that they dropped what they had in their hands; but the old

woman nodding her head, said, " Ah, you dear children, what has brought you here? Come in and stop with me, and no harm shall come to you; " and so saying she took them both by the hand, and led them into her cottage. A good meal of milk and pancakes, with sugar, apples, and nuts, was spread on the table, and in the back room were two nice little beds, covered with white, where Hansel and Grethel laid themselves down, and thought themselves in heaven. The old woman behaved very kindly to them, but in reality she was a wicked old witch who waylaid children, and built the breadhouse in order to entice them in; but as soon as they were in her power she killed them, cooked and ate them, and made a great festival of the day. Witches have red eyes, and cannot see very far; but they have a fine sense of smelling, like wild beasts, so that they know when children approach them. When Hansel and Grethel came near the witch's house she laughed wickedly, saying, " Here come two who shall not escape me." And early in the morning, before they awoke, she went up to them, and saw how lovingly they lay sleeping, with their chubby red cheeks; and she mumbled to herself, " That will be a good bite." Then she took up Hansel with her rough hand, and shut him in a little cage with a lattice-door; and although he screamed loudly it was of no use. Grethel came next, and shaking her till she awoke, she said, " Get up, you lazy thing, and fetch some water to cook something good for your brother, who must remain in that stall and get fat; and when he is fat enough I shall eat him." Grethel began to cry, but it was all useless, for the old witch made her do as she wanted. So a nice meal was cooked for Hansel, but Grethel got nothing else but a crab's claw.

Every morning the old witch came to the cage and said, " Hansel, stretch out your finger that I may feel whether you are getting fat."

But Hansel used to stretch out a bone, and the old woman, having very bad sight, thought it was his finger, and wondered very much why he did not fatten. When four weeks had passed, and Hansel still kept quite lean, she lost all her patience, and would not wait any longer.

"Grethel," she cried in a passion, "get some water quickly; be Hansel fat or lean, this morning I will kill and cook him."

Oh, how the poor little sister grieved, as she was forced to fetch the water, and fast the tears ran down her cheeks! "Dear good God, help us now!" she prayed. "Had we only been eaten by the wild beasts in the wood, then we should have died together."

But the old witch called out, "Leave off that noise; it will not help you a bit."

So early in the morning Grethel was compelled to go out and fill the kettle, and make a fire.

"First, we will bake, however," said the old woman; "I have already heated the oven and kneaded the dough;" and so saying, she pushed poor Grethel up to the oven, out of which the flames were burning fiercely. "Creep in," said the witch, "and see if it is hot enough, and then we will put in the bread;" but she intended when Grethel got in, to shut up the oven and let her bake, so that she might eat her as well as Hansel. Grethel perceived her wicked thoughts, and

said, " I do not
know how to do
it : how shall I
get in ?" " You
stupid goose,"
said she, " the
opening is big
enough. See, I
could even get
in myself !" and
she went and
put her head
into the oven.
Then Grethel
gave her a push,
so that she fell
right in, and
shutting the

iron door Grethel bolted it. Oh ! how horribly the witch howled ;
but the little girl ran away, and left her to burn to ashes.

Now she hastened to Hansel, and, opening the door, called
out, " Hansel, we are saved ; the old witch is dead ! "

So he sprang out, like a bird from his cage when the door is
opened ; and they were so glad that they fell upon each other's neck,
and kissed each other over and over again.

And now, as there was nothing to fear, they went back to the
witch's house, where in every corner were caskets full of pearls and
precious stones.

" These are better than pebbles," said Hansel, putting as many
into his pocket as it would hold ; while Grethel thought, " I will
take some home too," and filled her apron full.

" We must be off now," said Hansel, " and get out of this
enchanted forest ;" but when they had walked for two hours they
came to a large piece of water.

" We cannot get over," said Hansel ; " I can see no bridge
at all."

" And there is no boat either," said Grethel, " but there swims a white Duck, I will ask her to help us over ; " and she sang,

> " Little Duck, good little Duck,
>   Grethel and Hansel, together we stand ;
> There is neither stile nor bridge,
>   Take us on your back to land."

So the Duck came to them, and Hansel sat himself on, and bade his sister sit beside him. " No," replied Grethel, " that will be too much for the Duck, she shall take us over one at a time." This the good little bird did, and when both were happily arrived on the other side, and had gone a little way, they came to a familiar wood, which they knew the better every step they went, and at last they perceived their own home. Then they began to run, and rushing into the house, they fell on their father's neck. He had not had one happy hour since he had left the children in the forest ; and his wife was dead. Grethel shook her apron, and the pearls and precious stones rolled upon the floor, and Hansel threw down one handful after the other out of his pocket. Then all their sorrows were ended and they lived together in great happiness.

My tale is done. There runs a mouse ; whoever catches her may make a great, great, large cap out of her fur.

BRIAR ROSE

ONCE upon a time there lived a king and queen who had no
children; and this they lamented very much.   But one day, as the
queen was walking by the side of the river, a little fish lifted its
head out of the water, and said, " Your wish shall be fulfilled, and
you shall soon have a daughter."

What the little fish had foretold soon came to pass; and the
queen had a little girl that was so very beautiful that the king could
not cease looking on her for joy, and determined to hold a great
feast.   So he invited not only his relations, friends, and neighbours,
but also all the fairies, that they might be kind and good to his little
daughter.   Now there were thirteen fairies in his kingdom, and he
had only twelve golden dishes for them to eat out of, so that he was

obliged to leave one of the fairies without an invitation. The rest
came, and after the feast was over they gave all their best gifts to
the little princess; one gave her virtue, another beauty, another
riches, and so on till she had all that was excellent in the world.
When eleven had done blessing her, the thirteenth, who had not
been invited, and was very angry on that account, came in, and
determined to take her revenge. So she cried out, "The king's
daughter shall in her fifteenth year be wounded by a spindle, and
fall down dead." Then the twelfth, who had not yet given her
gift, came forward and said that the bad wish must be fulfilled, but
that she could soften it, and that the king's daughter should not die,
but fall asleep for a hundred years.

But the king hoped to save his dear child from the threatened
evil, and ordered that all the spindles in the kingdom should be
bought up and destroyed. All the fairies' gifts were in the
meantime fulfilled; for the princess was so beautiful, and well-
behaved, and amiable, and wise, that everyone who knew her
loved her.

Now it happened that on the very day she was fifteen years
old the king and queen were not at home, and she was left alone in
the palace. So she roamed about by herself, and looked at all the
rooms and chambers, till at last she came to an old tower, to which
there was a narrow staircase ending with a little door. In the door
there was a golden key, and when she turned it the door sprang
open, and there sat an old lady spinning away very busily.

"Why, how now, good mother," said the princess, "what are
you doing there?"

"Spinning," said the old lady, and nodded her head.

"How prettily that little thing turns round!" said the princess,
and took the spindle and began to spin. But scarcely had she
touched it before the prophecy was fulfilled, and she fell down
lifeless on the ground.

However, she was not dead, but had only fallen into a deep
sleep; and the king and the queen, who just then came home, and
all their court, fell asleep too, and the horses slept in the stables, and
the dogs in the yard, the pigeons on the house-top, and the flies on

the walls. Even the fire on the hearth left off blazing, and went to sleep; and the meat that was roasting stood still; and the cook, who was at that moment pulling the kitchen - boy by the hair to give him a box on the ear for something he had done amiss, let him go, and both fell asleep; and so everything stood still, and slept soundly.

A high hedge of thorns soon grew around the palace, and every year it became higher and thicker, till at last the whole palace was surrounded and hidden, so that not even the roof or the chimneys could be seen.

But there went a report through all the land of the beautiful sleeping Briar Rose, for thus was the king's daughter called; so that from time to time several kings' sons came, and tried to break through the thicket into the palace.

This they could never do; for the thorns and bushes laid

hold of them as it were with hands, and there they stuck fast and died miserably.

After many, many years there came another king's son into that land, and an old man told him the story of the thicket of thorns, and how a beautiful palace stood behind it, in which was a wondrous princess, called Briar Rose, asleep with all her court. He told, too, how he had heard from his grandfather that many, many princes had come, and had tried to break through the thicket, but had stuck fast and died.

Then the young prince said, " All this shall not frighten me ; I will go and see Briar Rose." The old man tried to dissuade him, but he persisted in going.

Now that very day were the hundred years completed ; and as the prince came to the thicket he saw nothing but beautiful flowering shrubs, through which he passed with ease, and they closed after him as firm as ever.

Then he came at last to the palace, and there in the yard lay the dogs asleep, and the horses in the stables, and on the roof sat the pigeons fast asleep with their heads under their wings ; and when he came into the palace, the flies slept on the walls, and the cook in the kitchen was still holding up her hand as if she would beat the boy, and the maid sat with a black fowl in her hand ready to be plucked.

Then he went on still further, and all was so still that he could hear every breath he drew ; till at last he came to the old tower and opened the door of the little room in which Briar Rose was, and there she lay fast asleep, and looked so beautiful that he could not take his eyes off, and he stooped down and gave her a kiss. But the moment he kissed her she opened her eyes and awoke, and smiled upon him.

Then they went out together, and presently the king and queen also awoke, and all the court, and they gazed on each other with great wonder.

And the horses got up and shook themselves, and the dogs jumped about and barked ; the pigeons took their heads from under their wings, and looked about and flew into the fields ; the

HANSEL AND GRETHEL

SNOW-WHITE AND ROSE-RED

flies on the walls buzzed away; the fire in the kitchen blazed up
and cooked the dinner, and the roast meat turned round again? the
cook gave the boy the box on his ear so that he cried out, and the
maid went on plucking the fowl.

And then was the wedding of the prince and Briar Rose
celebrated, and they lived happily together all their lives long.

SNOW-WHITE
AND
ROSE-RED

A POOR widow once lived in a little cottage. In front of the cottage was a garden, in which were growing two rose trees; one of these bore white roses, and the other red.

She had two children, who resembled the rose trees. One was called Snow-White, and the other Rose-Red; and they were as religious and loving, busy and untiring, as any two children ever were.

Snow-White was more gentle, and quieter than her sister, who liked better skipping about the fields, seeking flowers, and catching summer birds; while Snow-White stayed at home with her mother, either helping her in her work, or, when that was done, reading aloud.

The two children had the greatest affection the one for the other. They were always seen hand in hand; and should Snow-White say to her sister, "We will never separate," the other would reply, "Not while we live," the mother adding, "That which one has, let her always share with the other."

They constantly ran together in the woods, collecting ripe berries; but not a single animal would have injured them; quite the reverse, they all felt the greatest esteem for the young creatures. The hare came to eat parsley from their hands, the deer grazed by their side, the stag bounded past them unheeding; the birds, likewise, did not stir from the bough, but sang in entire security. No mischance befell them; if benighted in the wood, they lay down on the moss to repose and sleep till the morning; and their mother was satisfied as to their safety, and felt no fear about them.

Once, when they had spent the night in the wood, and the bright sunrise awoke them, they saw a beautiful child, in a snow-white robe, shining like diamonds, sitting close to the spot where they had reposed. She arose when they opened their eyes, and looked kindly at them; but said no word, and passed from their sight into the wood. When the children looked around they saw they had been sleeping on the edge of a precipice, and would surely have fallen over if they had gone forward two steps further in the darkness. Their mother said the beautiful child must have been the angel who keeps watch over good children.

Snow-White and Rose-Red kept their mother's cottage so clean that it gave pleasure only to look in. In summer-time Rose-Red attended to the house, and every morning, before her mother awoke, placed by her bed a bouquet which had in it a rose from each of the rose-trees. In winter-time Snow-White set light to the fire, and put on the kettle, after polishing it until it was like gold for brightness. In the evening, when snow was falling, her mother would bid her bolt the door, and then, sitting by the hearth, the good widow would read aloud to them from a big book while the little girls were spinning. Close by them lay a lamb, and a white pigeon, with its head tucked under its wing, was on a perch behind.

One evening, as they were all sitting cosily together like this, there was a knock at the door, as if someone wished to come in.

"Make haste, Rose-Red!" said her mother; "open the door; it is surely some traveller seeking shelter." Rose-Red accordingly pulled back the bolt, expecting to see some poor man. But it was nothing of the kind; it was a bear, that thrust his big black head in at the open door. Rose-Red cried out and sprang back, the lamb bleated, the dove fluttered her wings, and Snow-White hid herself behind her mother's bed. The bear began speaking, and said, " Do not be afraid ; I will not do you any harm ; I am half-frozen and would like to warm myself a little at your fire."

" Poor bear ! " the mother replied ; " come in and lie by the fire ; only be careful that your hair is not burnt." Then she called Snow-White and Rose-Red, telling them that the bear was kind, and would not harm them. They came, as she bade them, and presently the lamb and the dove drew near also without fear.

" Children," begged the bear ; " knock some of the snow off my coat." So they brought the broom and brushed the bear's coat quite clean.

After that he stretched himself out in front of the fire, and pleased himself by growling a little, only to show that he was happy and comfortable. Before long they were all quite good friends, and the children began to play with their unlooked-for visitor, pulling his thick fur, or placing their feet on his back, or rolling him over and over. Then they took a slender hazel-twig, using it upon his thick coat, and they laughed when he growled. The bear permitted them to amuse themselves in this way, only occasionally calling out, when it went a little too far, " Children, spare me an inch of life."

When it was night, and all were making ready to go to bed, the widow told the bear, " You may stay here and lie by the hearth, if you like, so that you will be sheltered from the cold and from the bad weather."

The offer was accepted, but when morning came, as the day broke in the east, the two children let him out, and over the snow he went back into the wood.

After this, every evening at the same time the bear came, lay by the fire, and allowed the children to play with him ; so they became quite fond of their curious playmate, and the door was not ever bolted in the evening until he had appeared.

When springtime came, and all around began to look green and bright, one morning the bear said to Snow-White, " Now I must leave you, and all the summer long I shall not be able to come back."

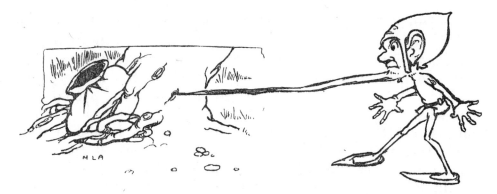

"Where, then, are you going, dear Bear?" asked Snow-White.

"I have to go to the woods to protect my treasure from the bad dwarfs. In winter-time, when the earth is frozen hard, they must remain underground, and cannot make their way through ; but now that the sunshine has thawed the earth they can come to the surface, and whatever gets into their hands, or is brought to their caves, seldom, if ever, again sees daylight."

Snow-White was very sad when she said good-bye to the good-natured beast, and unfastened the door, that he might go; but in going out he was caught by a hook in the lintel, and a scrap of his fur being torn, Snow-White thought there was something shining like gold through the rent; but he went out so quickly that she could not feel certain what it was, and soon he was hidden among the trees.

One day the mother sent her children into the wood to pick up sticks. They found a big tree lying on the ground. It had been felled, and towards the roots they noticed something skipping and springing, which they could not make out, as it was sometimes hidden in the grasses. As they came nearer they could see it was a dwarf, with a shrivelled-up face and a snow-white beard an ell long. The beard was fixed in a gash in the tree trunk, and the tiny fellow was hopping to and fro, like a dog at the end of a string, but he could not manage to free himself. He stared at the children with his red, fiery eyes, and called out, "Why are you standing there? Can't you come and try to help me?"

"What were you doing, little fellow?" enquired Rose-Red.

"Stupid, inquisitive goose!" replied the dwarf; "I meant to split the trunk, so that I could chop it up for kitchen sticks; big logs would burn up the small quantity of food we cook, for people like us do not consume great heaps of food, as you heavy, greedy folk do. The bill-hook I had driven in, and soon I should have done what I required; but the tool suddenly sprang from the cleft which so quickly shut up again that it caught my handsome white beard; and here I must stop, for I cannot set myself free. You stupid palefaced creatures! You laugh, do you?"

In spite of the dwarf's bad temper, the girls took all possible pains to release the little man, but without avail; the beard could not be moved, it was wedged too tightly.

"I will run and get someone else," said Rose-Red.

"Idiot!" cried the dwarf. "Who would go and get more people? Already there are two too many. Can't you think of something better?"

"Don't be so impatient," said Snow-White. "I will try to think." She clapped her hands as if she had discovered a remedy, took out her scissors, and in a moment set the dwarf free by cutting off the end of his beard.

Immediately the dwarf felt that he was free he seized a sack full of gold that was hidden amongst the tree's roots, and, lifting it up, grumbled out, "Clumsy creatures, to cut off a bit of my beautiful beard, of which I am so proud! I leave the cuckoos to pay you for what you did." Saying this, he swung the sack across his shoulder, and went off, without even casting a glance at the children.

Not long afterwards the two sisters went to angle in the brook, meaning to catch fish for dinner. As they were drawing near the water they perceived something, looking like a large grasshopper, springing towards the stream, as if it were going in. They hurried up to see what it might be, and found that it was the dwarf. "Where are you going?" said Rose-Red. "Surely you will not jump into the water?"

"I'm not such a simpleton as that!" yelled the little man. "Don't you see that a wretch of a fish is pulling me in?"

The dwarf had been sitting angling from the side of the stream when, by ill-luck, the wind had entangled his beard in his line, and just afterwards a big fish taking the bait, the unamiable little fellow had not sufficient strength to pull it out; so the fish had the advantage, and was dragging the dwarf after it. Certainly, he caught at every stalk and spray near him, but that did not assist him greatly; he was forced to follow all the twistings of the fish, and was perpetually in danger of being drawn into the brook.

The girls arrived just in time. They caught hold of him firmly and endeavoured to untwist his beard from the line, but in vain; they were too tightly entangled. There was nothing left but again to make use of the scissors; so they were taken out, and the tangled portion was cut off

When the dwarf noticed what they were about, he exclaimed, in a great rage, " Is this how you damage my beard? Not content with making it shorter before, you are now making it still smaller, and completely spoiling it. I shall not ever dare show my face to my friends. I wish you had missed your way before you took this road." Then he fetched a sack of pearls that lay among the rushes, and, not saying another word, hobbled off and disappeared behind a large stone.

Soon after this it chanced that the poor widow sent her children to the town to purchase cotton, needles, ribbon, and tape. The way to the town ran over a common, on which in every direction large masses of rocks were scattered about. The children's attention was soon attracted to a big bird that hovered in the air. They remarked that, after circling slowly for a time, and gradually getting nearer to the ground, it all of a sudden pounced down amongst a mass of rock. Instantly a heartrending cry reached their ears, and, running quickly, to the place they saw, with horror, that the eagle had seized their former acquaintance, the dwarf, and was just about to carry him off. The kind children did not hesitate for an instant. They took a firm hold of the little man, and strove so stoutly with the eagle for possession of his contemplated prey, that, after much rough treatment on both sides, the dwarf was left in the hands of his brave little friends, and the eagle took to flight.

As soon as the little man had in some measure recovered from his alarm, his small squeaky, cracked voice was heard saying, "Couldn't you have held me more gently? See my little coat; you have rent and damaged it in a fine manner, you clumsy, officious things!" Then he picked up a sack of jewels, and slipped out of sight behind a piece of rock.

The maidens by this time were quite used to his ungrateful, ungracious ways; so they took no notice of it, but went on their way, made their purchases, and then were ready to return to their happy home.

On their way back, suddenly, once more they ran across their dwarf friend. Upon a clear space he had turned out his sack of jewels, so that he could count and admire them, for he had not imagined that anybody would at so late an hour be coming across the common.

The setting sun was shining upon the brilliant stones, and their changing hues and sparkling rays caused the children to pause to admire them also.

"What are you

gazing at?" cried the dwarf, at the same time becoming red with rage; "and what are you standing there for, making ugly faces?"

It is probable that he might have proceeded in the same complimentary manner, but suddenly a great growl was heard near by them, and a big black bear joined the party. Up jumped the dwarf in extremest terror, but could not get to his hiding-place, the bear was too close to him; so he cried out in very evident anguish—

"Dear Mr. Bear, forgive me, I pray! I will render to you all my treasure. Just see those precious stones lying there! Grant me my life! What would you do with such an insignificant little fellow? You would not notice me between your teeth. See, though, those two children, they would be delicate morsels, and are as plump as partridges; I beg of you to take them, good Mr. Bear, and let me go!"

But the bear would not be moved by his speeches. He gave the ill-disposed creature a blow with his paw, and he lay lifeless on the ground.

Meanwhile the maidens were running away, making off for home as well as they could; but all of a sudden they were stopped by a well-known voice that called out, "Snow-White, Rose-Red, stay! Do not fear. I will accompany you."

The bear quickly came towards them, but, as he reached their side, suddenly the bear-skin slipped to the ground, and there before them was standing a handsome man, completely garmented in gold, who said—

"I am a king's son, who was enchanted by the wicked dwarf lying over there. He stole my treasure, and compelled me to roam the woods transformed into a big bear until his death should set me free. Therefore he has only received a well-deserved punishment."

Some time afterwards Snow-White married the Prince, and Rose-Red his brother.

They shared between them the enormous treasure which the dwarf had collected in his cave.

The old mother spent many happy years with her children. The two rose-trees she took with her when she left the cottage, and they grew in front of her window, where they continued to bear each year the most beautiful roses, white and red.

THE TRAVELS

OF

TOM THUMB

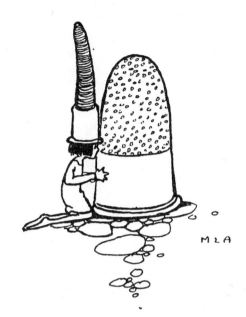

THERE lived a tailor who had only one son, and he was extremely small, not any larger than your thumb, and so was called Tom Thumb.

However, he was a courageous little fellow, and he told his father, "Father, I am determined to go into the world to seek my fortune."

"Very well, my son," answered the old man, and taking a big darning needle, he made a top to it of sealing wax, and gave it to Tom Thumb, saying:

"There is a sword for you to use to defend yourself on your journeyings."

Then the little fellow, desiring to dine once more with his parents, popped into the kitchen to find out what his mother was preparing for his last dinner at home. All the dishes were ready to be taken in, and they were standing upon the hearth.

"What is it you have for dinner, dear mother?" he enquired.

"You can look for yourself," she replied.

Then Tom sprang up on to the hob, and peeped into all the

dishes, but over one he leant so far, that he was carried up by the steam through the chimney, and then for some distance he floated on the smoke, but after a while he fell upon the ground once more.

Now, at last, Tom Thumb was really out in the wide world, and he went on cheerily, and after a time was engaged by a master tailor; but here the food was not so good as his mother's, and it was not to his taste.

So he said, " Mistress, if you will not give me better things to eat, I shall chalk upon your door, ' Too many potatoes, and not enough meat.   Good-bye, potato-mill.' "

" I should like to know what you want, you little grasshopper ! " cried the woman very angrily, and she seized a shred of cloth to strike him; however, the tiny tailor popped under a thimble, and from it he peeped, putting out his tongue at the mistress.

So she took up the thimble meaning to catch him, but Tom Thumb hid himself amongst the shreds of cloth, and when she began to search through those, he slipped into a crack in the table, but put out his head to laugh at her ; so she tried again to hit him with the shred, but did not succeed in doing so, for he slipped through the crack into the table drawer.

At last though, he was caught, and driven out of the house.

So the little fellow continued his travels, and presently, entering a thick forest, he encountered a company of robbers who were plotting to steal the king's treasure.

As soon as they saw the little tailor, they said to themselves, " A little fellow like this could creep through a keyhole, and aid us greatly."   So one called out,

" Hullo, little man, will you come with us to the king's treasury?   Certainly a Goliath like you could creep in with ease, and throw out the coins to us."

After considering awhile, Tom Thumb consented, and accompanied them to the king's treasury.

From top to bottom they inspected the door to discover a crack large enough for him to get through, and soon found one. He was for going in directly, but one of the sentinels happening to catch sight of him, exclaimed: "Here is indeed an ugly spider; I will crush it with my foot."

"Leave the poor creature alone," the other said; "it has not done you any harm."

So Tom Thumb slipped through the crack, and made his way to the treasury. Then he opened the window, and cast out the coins to the robbers who were waiting below. While the little tailor was engaged in this exciting employment, he heard the king coming to inspect his treasure, so as quickly as possible, he crept out of sight. The king noticed that his treasure had been disarranged, and soon observed that coins were missing; but he was utterly unable to think how they could have been stolen, for the locks and bolts had not been tampered with, and everything was well fastened.

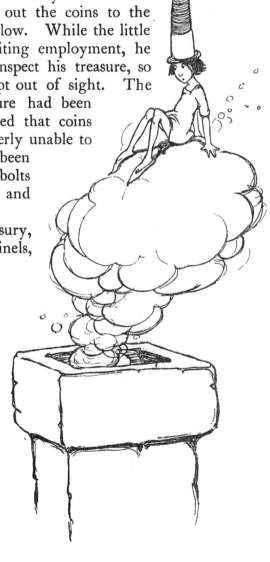

On going from the treasury, he warned the two sentinels, saying:

"Be on the watch, some one is after the money," and quite soon, on Tom Thumb setting to work again, they heard very clearly the coins ringing, chink, chank, as they struck one against the other.

As quickly as possible they unfastened the building and went in, hoping to take the thief.

But Tom Thumb was too quick for them, he sprang into a corner, and hiding himself behind a coin, so that nothing of him was visible, he made fun of the sentinels; crying "I am here!" Then when the men hurried to the spot, where the voice came from, he was no longer there, but from a different place cried out: "Ha, Ha! here I am!"

So the sentinels kept jumping about, but so cleverly did Tom move from one spot to another, that they were obliged to run around the whole time, hoping to find somebody, until at length, quite tired out, they went off.

Then Tom Thumb went on with his work, and one after another he threw all the coins out of the window, but the very last he sounded and rang with all his might and springing nimbly upon it, so flew through the window.

The robbers were loud in their praises.

"Indeed you are a brave fellow," they said, "will you be our captain?"

Tom Thumb, thanking them, declined this honour, for he was anxious to see more of the world. Then the booty was apportioned out, but only a ducat was given to the little tailor, for that was as much as he could carry.

So Tom girded on his sword again, and bidding farewell to the robbers, continued his travels.

He tried to get work under various masters, but they would have nothing to do with him, so after a while he took service at an inn. But the maids there disliked him, for he was about everywhere, and saw all that went on, without being seen himself; and he told their mistress of their dishonest ways, of what was taken off the plates, and from out the cellars.

So they threatened they would drown him, if they caught him, and determined to do him some harm. Then, one day, a maid mowing in the garden, saw Tom Thumb running in and out between the blades of grass, so she cut the grass, in great haste, just where he chanced to be, tied it all in a bundle, and, without anyone knowing, threw it to the cows.

Then one big black cow took up a mouthful of grass directly, with Tom in it, and swallowed it down; without doing him any damage, however.

But Tom did not approve of his position, for it was pitch dark down there, with no light burning.

When milking time came, he shouted:

> "Drip, drap, drop,
> Will the milking soon stop?"

but the sound of the milk, trickling into the pail, prevented his voice being heard.

Not long afterwards the master came into the shed, and said: "I will have that cow killed to-morrow."

This put Tom Thumb into a great fright, and he called out loudly: "Please let me out, here I am inside."

This the master heard plainly enough, but could not make out where the voice came from.

"Where are you?" he enquired.

"In the black cow," was the reply.

However the master could not understand what was meant, and so went away.

The following morning the cow was killed, but fortunately in the cutting up, the knife did not touch Tom Thumb, who was put aside with the meat that was to be made into sausages.

When the butcher began chopping, he cried as loudly as he could :

" Don't chop far, I am down beneath," but the chopper made so much noise, that he attracted no attention.

It was indeed a terrible situation for poor Tom. But being in danger brightens one's wits, and he sprang so nimbly, this way and that, keeping clear of the chopper, that not a blow struck him, and he did not get even a scratch.

However he could not escape, there was no help for it, he was forced into a skin with the sausage meat, so was compelled to make himself as comfortable as might be. It was very close quarters, and besides that, the sausages were suspended to smoke in the chimney, which was by no means entertaining, and the time passed slowly.

When winter came, he was taken down for a guest's meal, and when the hostess was slicing the sausage he had to be on his guard, lest if he stretched out his head it might be cut off.

Watching his opportunity, at last he was able to jump out of the sausage, and right glad was he to be once again in the company of his fellow-men.

It was not very long, however, that he stayed in this house, where he had been met by so many misfortunes, and again he set forth on his travels, rejoicing in his freedom, but

this did not long con-
tinue.

Swiftly running across the
field came a fox, who, in an
instant had snapped up poor
little Tom.

"Oh, Mr. Fox," called out
the little tailor, "it is I who
am in your throat; please let
me out."

"Certainly," answered
Reynard,
"you are
not a bit
better than
nothing at
all, you
don't in the
least satisfy
me; make
me a pro-
mise, that
I shall have
the hens in
your father's
yard, and
you shall
regain your
liberty."

M.L.A.

"Willingly, you shall have all the hens; I make you a
faithful promise," responded Tom Thumb.

So the fox coughed and set him free, and himself carried
Tom home.

Then when the father had his dear little son once more, he
gave the fox all his hens, with the greatest of pleasure.

"Here, father, I am bringing you a golden coin from my

travels," said the little fellow, and he brought out the ducat the thieves had apportioned to him.

"But how was it that the fox was given all the poor little hens?" "Foolish little one, don't you think your father would rather have you, than all the hens he ever had in his yard?"

THE GOOSE-GIRL

AN old queen, whose husband had been dead some years, had a beautiful daughter. When she grew up, she was betrothed to a prince who lived a great way off; and as the time drew near for her to be married, she got ready to set off on her journey to his country. Then the queen, her mother, packed up a great many costly things—jewels, and gold, and silver; trinkets, fine dresses, and in short, everything that became a royal bride; for she loved her child very dearly: and she gave her a waiting-maid to ride with her, and give her into the bridegroom's hands; and each had a horse for the journey. Now the princess's horse was called Falada, and could speak.

When the time came for them to set out, the old queen went into her bed-chamber, and took a little knife, and cut off a lock of her hair, and gave it to her daughter, saying, " Take care of it, dear child; for it is a charm that may be of use to you on the road." Then they took a sorrowful leave of each other, and the princess put the lock of her mother's hair into her bosom, got upon her horse, and set off on her journey to her bridegroom's kingdom.

One day, as they were riding along by the side of a brook, the princess began to feel very thirsty, and said to her maid, " Pray get down and fetch me some water in my golden cup out of yonder brook, for I want to drink." "Nay," said the maid, "if you are thirsty, get down yourself, and lie down by the water and drink; I shall not be your waiting-maid any longer." The princess was so thirsty that she got down, and knelt over the little brook and drank, for she was frightened, and dared not bring out her golden cup; and then she wept, and said, " Alas! what will become of me?" And the lock of hair answered her, and said—

> " Alas! alas! if thy mother knew it,
> Sadly, sadly her heart would rue it."

But the princess was very humble and meek, so she said nothing to her maid's ill behaviour, but got upon her horse again.

Then all rode further on their journey, till the day grew so warm, and the sun so scorching, that the bride began to feel very thirsty again; and at last, when they came to a river, she forgot her maid's rude speech, and said, " Pray get down and fetch me some water to drink in my golden cup." But the maid answered her, and even spoke more haughtily than before, " Drink if you will, but I shall not be your waiting-maid." Then the princess was so thirsty that she got off her horse and lay down, and held her head over the running stream, and cried, and said, " What will become of me?" And the lock of hair answered her again—

> " Alas! alas! if thy mother knew it,
> Sadly, sadly her heart would rue it."

And as she leaned down to drink, the lock of hair fell from her

bosom and floated away with the water, without her seeing it, she
was so much frightened. But her maid saw it, and was very glad, for
she knew the charm, and saw that the poor bride would be in her
power now that she had lost the hair. So when the bride had finished
drinking, and would have got upon Falada again, the maid said,
"I shall ride upon Falada, and you may have my horse instead;"
so she was forced to give up her horse, and soon afterwards to take
off her royal clothes, and
put on her maid's shabby
ones.

At last, as they drew
near the end of the jour-
ney, this treacherous servant threatened to kill
her mistress if she ever
told anyone what had
happened. But Falada
saw it all, and marked it
well. Then the waiting-
maid got upon
Falada, and the real
bride was set upon
the other horse, and
they went on in this
way till at
last they
came to the
royal court.
There was
great joy at
their com-
ing, and
the prince
hurried to
meet them,
and lifted

MABEL
LUCIE
ATTWELL.

the maid from her horse, thinking she was the one who was to be his
wife; and she was led upstairs to the royal chamber, but the true
princess was told to stay in the court below.

However the old king happened to be looking out of the
window, and saw her in the yard below; and as she looked very
pretty, and too delicate for a waiting-maid, he went into the royal
chamber to ask the bride whom it was she had brought with her, that
was thus left standing in the court below. "I brought her with me
for the sake of her company on the road," said she. "Pray give the
girl some work to do, that she may not be idle." The old king
could not for some time think of any work for her, but at last he
said, "I have a lad who takes care of my geese; she may go and
help him." Now the name of this lad, that the real bride was to
help in watching the king's geese, was Curdken.

Soon after, the false bride said to the prince, "Dear husband,
pray do me one piece of kindness." "That I will," said the prince.
"Then tell one of your slaughterers to cut off the head of the horse I
rode upon, for it was very unruly, and plagued me sadly on the
road." But the truth was, she was very much afraid lest Falada
should speak, and tell all she had done to the princess. She carried
her point, and the faithful Falada was killed; but when the true
princess heard of it she wept, and begged the man to nail up Falada's
head against a large dark gate in the city through which she had to
pass every morning and evening, that there she might still see him
sometimes. Then the slaughterer said he would do as she wished, so
he cut off the head and nailed it fast under the dark gate.

Early the next morning, as the princess and Curdken went out
through the gate, she said sorrowfully—

"Falada, Falada, there thou art hanging!"

and the head answered—

"Bride, bride, there thou art ganging!
Alas! alas! if thy mother knew it,
Sadly, sadly her heart would rue it."

Then they went out of the city, driving the geese. And when
they came to the meadow, the princess sat down upon a bank there,

and let down her waving locks of hair, which were all of pure gold; and when Curdken saw it glitter in the sun, he ran up, and would have pulled some of the locks out; but she cried—

" Blow, breezes, blow!
   Let Curdken's hat go!
   Blow, breezes, blow!
   Let him after it go!
   O'er hills, dales, and rocks,
   Away be it whirl'd,
   Till the golden locks
   Are all comb'd and curl'd!"

Then there came a wind, so strong that it blew off Curdken's hat, and away it flew over the hills, and he after it; till, by the time he came back, she had done combing and curling her hair, and put it up again safely. Then he was very angry and sulky, and would not speak to her at all; but they watched the geese until it grew dark in the evening, and then drove them homewards.

The next morning, as they were going through the dark gate, the poor girl looked up at Falada's head, and cried—

" Falada, Falada, there thou art hanging!"

and it answered—

> " Bride, bride, there thou art ganging !
> Alas ! alas ! if thy mother knew it,
> Sadly, sadly her heart would rue it."

Then she drove on the geese and sat down again in the meadow, and began to comb out her hair as before, and Curdken ran up to her, and wanted to take hold of it; but she cried out quickly—

> " Blow, breezes, blow !
> Let Curdken's hat go !
> Blow, breezes, blow !
> Let him after it go !
> O'er hills, dales, and rocks,
> Away be it whirl'd
> Till the golden locks
> Are all comb'd and curl'd !"

Then the wind came and blew off his hat, and off it flew a great distance over the hills and far away, so that he had to run after it: and when he came back, she had done up her hair again, and all was safe. So they watched the geese till it grew dark.

In the evening, after they came home, Curdken went to the old king, and said, "I cannot have that strange girl to help me to keep the geese any longer."

" Why ? " enquired the king.

" Because she does nothing but tease me all day long."

Then the king made him tell all that had passed.

And Curdken said, " When we go in the morning through the dark gate with our flock of geese, she weeps, and talks with the head of a horse that hangs upon the wall, and says—

> ' Falada, Falada, there thou art hanging !'

and the head answers—

> ' Bride, bride, there thou art ganging !
> Alas ! alas ! if thy mother knew it,
> Sadly, sadly her heart would rue it.' "

And Curdken went on telling the king what had happened upon the meadow where the geese fed; and how his hat was blown away, and he was forced to run after it, and leave his flock. But the old king

told him to go out again as usual the next
day: and when morning came, he placed
himself behind the dark gate, and heard
how the princess spoke, and how Falada
answered; and then he went into the field
and hid himself in a bush by the meadow's
side, and soon saw with his own eyes how
they drove the flock of geese, and how after
a little time, she let down her hair that glittered in the sun; and
then he heard her say—

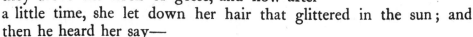

> " Blow, breezes, blow !
> Let Curdken's hat go !
> Blow, breezes, blow !
> Let him after it go !
> O'er hills, dales, and rocks
> Away be it whirl'd,
> Till the golden locks
> Are all comb'd and curl'd ! "

And soon came a gale of wind, and carried away Curdken's hat,
while the girl went on combing and curling her hair.

All this the old king saw: so he went home without being
seen; and when the goose-girl came back in the evening, he called
her aside, and asked her why she did so: but she burst into tears,
and said, " That I must not tell you or any man, or I shall lose
my life."

But the old king begged so hard that she had no peace till she
had told him all, word for word: and it was very lucky for her
that she did so, for the king ordered royal clothes to be put upon
her, and he gazed with wonder, she was so beautiful.

Then he called his son, and told him that he had only the false bride, for that she was merely a waiting maid, while the true one stood by.

And the young king rejoiced when he saw her beauty, and heard how meek and patient she had been; and without saying anything, he ordered a great feast to be prepared for all his court.

The bridegroom sat at the top, with the false princess on one side, and the true one on the other; but nobody knew her, for she was quite dazzling to their eyes, and was not at all like the little goose-girl, now that she had on her brilliant dress.

When they had eaten and drunk, and were very merry, the old king told all the story, as one that he had once heard of, and asked the true waiting-maid what she thought ought to be done to anyone who would behave thus.

"Nothing better," said this false bride, "than that she should be thrown into a cask stuck around with sharp nails, and that two white horses should

be put to it, and should drag it from street to street till she is dead."

"Thou art she!" said the old king; "and since thou hast judged thyself, it shall be so done to thee."

Then the young king was married to his true wife, and they reigned over the kingdom in peace and happiness all their lives.

CINDERELLA

THE wife of a rich man fell sick: and when she felt that her end drew nigh, she called her only daughter to her bed-side, and said, "Always be a good girl, and I will look down from heaven and watch over you." Soon afterwards she shut her eyes and died, and was buried in the garden; and the little girl went every day to her grave and wept, and was always good and kind to all about her. And the snow spread a beautiful white covering over the grave; but by the time the sun had melted it away again, her father had married another wife. This new wife had two daughters of her own, that she brought home with her: they were fair in face but foul at heart, and it was now a sorry time for the poor little girl. "What does the good-for-nothing thing want in the parlour?" said they; "they who would eat bread should first earn it; away with the kitchen maid!" Then they took away her fine clothes, and gave her an old frock to put on, and laughed at her and turned her into the kitchen.

Then she was forced to do hard work; to rise early, before

daylight, to bring the water, to make the fire, to cook and to wash. Besides that, the sisters plagued her in all sorts of ways and laughed at her.   In the evening when she was tired she had no bed to lie down on, but was made to lie by the hearth among the ashes; and then, as she was of course always dusty and dirty, they called her Cinderella.

It happened once that her father was going to the fair, and asked his wife's daughters what he should bring to them.   " Fine clothes," said the first.   " Pearls and diamonds," said the second.   " Now, child," said he to his own daughter, " what will you have?" " The first sprig, dear father, that rubs against your hat on your way home," said she.   Then he bought for the two first the fine clothes and pearls and diamonds they had asked for: and on his way home, as he rode through a green copse, a sprig of hazel brushed against him, and almost pushed off his hat, so he broke it off and brought it away; and when he got home he gave it to his daughter.   Then she took it, and went to her mother's grave and planted it there, and cried so much that it was watered with her tears; and there it grew and became a fine tree.   Three times every day she went to it and wept; and soon a little bird came and built its nest upon the tree, and talked with her and watched over her, and brought her whatever she wished for.

Now it happened that the king of the land held a feast which was to last three days, and out of those who came to it his son was to choose a bride for himself; and Cinderella's two sisters were asked to come.   So they called Cinderella, and said, " Now, comb our hair; brush our shoes, and tie our sashes for us, for we are going to dance at the king's feast."   Then she did as she was told, but when all was done she could not help crying, for she thought to herself, she would have liked to go to the dance too, and at last she begged her mother very hard to let her go.   " You! Cinderella?" said she; " you who have nothing to wear, no clothes at all, and who cannot even dance—you want to go to the ball?"   And when she kept on begging, to get rid of her, she said at last, " I will throw this basinful of peas into the ash heap, and if you have picked them all out in two hours' time you shall go to the feast too."   Then she threw the peas into the ashes; but the little maiden ran out at the back door into the garden, and cried out—

> " Hither, hither, through the sky,
> Turtle-doves and linnets, fly!
> Blackbird, thrush, and chaffinch gay,
> Hither, hither, haste away!
> One and all, come, help me quick!
> Haste ye, haste ye—pick, pick, pick!"

Then first came two white doves flying in at the kitchen window; and next came two turtle-doves; and after them all the little birds under heaven came chirping and fluttering in, and flew down into the ashes; and the little doves stooped their heads down and set to work, pick, pick, pick; and then the others began to pick, pick, pick, and picked out all the good grain and put it into a dish, and left the ashes. At the end of one hour the work was done, and all flew out again at the windows. Then she brought the dish to her mother, overjoyed at the thought that now she should go to the feast. But the mother said, "No, no! indeed, you have no clothes and cannot dance; you shall not go." And when Cinderella begged very hard to go, she said, "If you can in one hour's time pick two of these dishes of peas out of the ashes, you shall go too." And thus she thought she should at last get rid of her. So she shook two dishes of peas into the ashes; but the little maiden went out into the garden at the back of the house, and called as before—

> " Hither, hither, through the sky,
> Turtle-doves and linnets, fly!
> Blackbird, thrush, and chaffinch gay,
> Hither, hither, haste away!
> One and all, come, help me quick!
> Haste ye, haste ye—pick, pick, pick!"

Then first came two white doves in at the kitchen window; and next came the turtle doves; and after them all the little birds under heaven came chirping and hopping about, and flew down about the ashes; and the little doves put their heads down and set to work, pick, pick, pick; and then the others began to pick, pick,

pick; and they put all the good grain into the dishes, and left all the ashes. Before half an hour's time all was done, and out they flew again. And then Cinderella took the dishes to her mother, rejoicing to think that she should now go to the ball. But her mother said, " It is all of no use, you cannot go; you have no clothes, and cannot dance; and you would only put us to shame; " and off she went with her two daughters to the feast.

Now when all were gone, and nobody left at home, Cinderella went sorrowfully and sat down under the hazel-tree, and cried out—

> " Shake, shake, hazel-tree,
> Gold and silver over me ! "

Then her friend the bird flew out of the tree and brought a gold and silver dress for her, and slippers of spangled silk; and she put them on, and followed her sisters to the feast. But they did not know her, and thought it must be some strange princess, she looked so fine and beautiful in her rich clothes; and they never once thought of Cinderella, but took for granted that she was safe at home in the dust.

The king's son soon came up to her, and took her by the hand and danced with her and no one else; and he never left her hand, but when anyone else came to ask her to dance, he said, " This lady is dancing with me." Thus they danced till a late hour of the night, and then she wanted to go home; and the king's son said, " I shall go and take care of you to your home," for he wanted to see where the beautiful maid lived. But she slipped away from him unawares, and ran off towards home, and the prince followed her; then she jumped up into the pigeon-house and shut the door. So he waited till her father came home, and told him that the unknown maiden who had been at the feast had hidden herself in the pigeon-house. But when they had broken open the door they found no one within; and as they came back into the house, Cinderella lay, as she always did, in her dirty frock by the ashes, and her dim little lamp burnt in the corner; for she had run as quickly as she could through the pigeon-house and on to the hazel-tree, and had there taken off her beautiful clothes, and laid them beneath the tree, that the bird might carry them away; and had seated herself amid the ashes again in her little old frock.

The next day, when the feast was again held, and her father, mother, and sisters were gone, Cinderella went to the hazel-tree and said—

> "Shake, shake, hazel-tree,
> Gold and silver over me!"

And the bird came and brought a still finer dress than the one she had worn the day before. And when she came in it to the ball everyone wondered at her beauty; but the king's son, who was waiting for her, took her by the hand and danced with her; and, when anyone asked her to dance, he said as before, "This lady is dancing with me." When night came she wanted to go home; and the king's son went with her as before, that he might see what house she entered; but she sprang away from him all at once into the garden behind her father's house. In this garden stood a fine large pear tree full of ripe fruit; and Cinderella, not knowing where to hide herself, jumped up into it without being seen. Then the king's son could not find out where she was gone, but waited till her father came home, and said to him, "The unknown lady who danced with me has slipped away, and I think she must have sprung into the pear-tree." The father thought to himself, "Can it be Cinderella?" So he ordered an axe to be brought, and they cut down the tree, but found no one upon it. And when they came back into the kitchen, there lay Cinderella in the ashes as usual; for she had slipped down on the other side of the tree, and carried her beautiful clothes back to the bird at the hazel-tree, and then put on her little old frock.

The third day, when her father and mother and sisters were gone, she went again into the garden, and said—

> "Shake, shake, hazel-tree,
> Gold and silver over me!"

Then her kind friend the bird brought a dress still finer than the former one, and slippers which were all of gold; so that, when she came to the feast, no one knew what to say for wonder at her

LITTLE RED-CAP

THE SIX SWANS

beauty; and the king's son danced with her alone, and when anyone else asked her to dance, he said, "This lady is my partner." Now when night came she wanted to go home; and the king's son would go with her, and said to himself, "I will not lose her this time;" but, however, she managed to slip away from him, though in such a hurry that she dropped her left golden slipper upon the stairs.

So the prince took the shoe, and went the next day to the king, his father, and said, "I will take for my wife the lady that this golden shoe fits."

Then both the sisters were overjoyed to hear this; for they had beautiful feet, and had no doubt that they could wear the golden slipper. The eldest went first into the room where the slipper was, and wanted to try it on, and the mother stood by. But her big toe could not go into it, and the shoe was altogether much too small for her. Then the mother gave her a knife, and said, "Never mind, cut it off. When you are queen you will not care about toes; you will not want to go on foot." So the silly girl cut her big toe off, and squeezed the shoe on, and went to the king's son. Then he took her for his bride, and set her beside him on his horse, and rode away with her.

But on their way home they had to pass by the hazel-tree that Cinderella had planted, and there sat a little dove on the branch, singing—

> "Back again! back again! look to the shoe!
> The shoe is too small, and not made for you!
> Prince! prince! look again for thy bride,
> For she's not the true one that sits by thy side."

Then the prince got down and looked at her foot, and saw by the blood that streamed from it, what a trick she had played him. So he turned his horse round, and brought the false bride back to her home, and said, "This is not the right bride; let the other sister try and put on the slipper." Then she went into the room and got her foot into the shoe, all but the heel, which was too large. But her mother squeezed it in till the blood came, and took her to the king's son; and he set her, as his bride, by his side on his horse, and rode away with her. But when they came to the hazel-tree, the little dove sat there still, and sang—

> "Back again! back again! look to the shoe!
> The shoe is too small, and not made for you!
> Prince! prince! look again for thy bride,
> For she's not the true one that sits by thy side."

Then he looked down, and saw that the blood streamed so

from the shoe that her white stockings were quite red. So he
turned his horse and brought her back again also.   "This is not the
true bride," said he to the father; "have you no other daughters?"
"No," said he; "there is only a little dirty Cinderella here, the
child of my first wife; I am sure she cannot be the bride."
However, the prince told him to send her.   But the mother said,
"No, no; she is much too dirty, she will not dare to show herself."
However, the prince would have her come.   And she first washed
her face and hands, and then went in and curtsied to him, and he
held out to her the golden slipper.

Then she took her clumsy shoe off her left foot, and put on
the golden slipper, and it fitted her as if it had been made for her.

And when he drew near and looked at her face he knew her, and said, " This is the right bride."

But the mother and both the sisters were frightened, and turned pale with anger as he took Cinderella on his horse, and rode away with her.   And when they came to the hazel-tree, the white dove sang—

> " Home ! home ! look at the shoe !
> Princess ! the shoe was made for you !
> Prince ! prince ! take home thy bride,
> For she is the true one that sits by thy side ! "

And when the dove had done its song, it came flying and perched upon her right shoulder, and so went home with her.

LITTLE

RED-CAP

MANY years ago there lived a dear little girl, who was beloved by every one who knew her; but her grandmother was so very fond of her that she never felt she could think and do enough to please this dear grand-daughter, and she presented the little girl with a red silk cap, which suited her so well, that she would never wear anything else, and so was called Little Red-Cap.

One day Red-Cap's mother said to her, " Come, Red-Cap, here is a nice piece of meat, and a bottle of wine: take these to your grandmother; she is weak and ailing, and they will do her good. Be there before she gets up; go quietly and carefully; and do not run, or you may fall and break the bottle, and then your grand-mother will get nothing. When you go into her room, do not forget to say ' Good-morning;' and do not pry into all the corners."

"I will do just as you say," answered Red-Cap, bidding good-bye to her mother.

The grandmother lived far away in the wood, a long walk from the village, and as Little Red-Cap came among the trees she met a Wolf; but she did not know what a wicked animal it was, and so she was not at all frightened. "Good-morning, Little Red-Cap," he said.

"Thank you, Mr. Wolf," said she.

"Where are you going so early, Little Red-Cap?"

"To my grandmother's," she answered.

"And what are you carrying in that basket?"

"Some wine and meat," she replied. "We baked the meat yesterday, so that grandmother, who is very weak, might have a nice strengthening meal."

"And where does your grandmother live?" asked the Wolf.

"Oh, quite twenty minutes' walk further in the forest. The cottage stands under three great oak trees; and close by are some nut bushes, by which you will at once know it."

The Wolf was thinking to himself, "She is a nice tender thing, and will taste better than the old woman; I must act cleverly, that I may make a meal of both."

Presently he came up again to Little Red-Cap, and said, "Just look at the beautiful flowers which grow around you; why do you not look about you? I believe you don't hear how sweetly the birds are singing. You walk as if you were going to school; see how cheerful everything is

about you in the forest."

And Little Red-Cap opened her eyes; and when she saw how the sunbeams glanced and danced through the trees, and what bright flowers were blooming in her path, she thought, "If I take my grandmother a fresh nosegay, she will be very much pleased; and it is so very early that I can, even then, get there in good time;" and running into the forest, she looked about for

flowers. But when she had once begun she did not know how to leave off, and kept going deeper and deeper amongst the trees looking for some still more beautiful flower. The Wolf, however, ran straight to the house of the old grandmother, and knocked at the door.

"Who's there?" asked the old lady.

"Only Little Red-Cap, bringing you some meat and wine; please open the door," answered the Wolf.

"Lift up the latch," cried the grandmother; "I am much too ill to get up myself."

So the Wolf lifted the latch, and the door flew open; and without a word, he jumped on to the bed, and gobbled up the poor

old lady.   Then he put on her clothes, and tied her night-cap over his head; got into the bed, and drew the blankets over him.   All this time Red-Cap was gathering flowers; and when she had picked as many as she could carry, she thought of her grandmother, and hurried to the cottage. She wondered greatly to find the door open; and when she got into the room, she began to feel very ill, and exclaimed, "How sad I feel!   I wish I had not come to-day."   Then she said, "Good morning," but received no reply; so she went up to the bed, and drew back the curtains, and there lay her grandmother, as she imagined, with the cap drawn half over her eyes, and looking very fierce.

"Oh, grandmother, what great ears you have!" she said.

"All the better to hear you with," was the reply.

"And what great eyes you have!"

"All the better to see you with."

"And what great hands you have!"

"All the better to touch you with."

"But, grandmother, what very great teeth you have!"

"All the better to eat you with;" and hardly were the words spoken when the Wolf made a jump out of bed, and swallowed up poor Little Red-Cap also.

As soon as the Wolf had thus satisfied his hunger, he laid himself down again on the bed, and went to sleep and snored very loudly. A huntsman passing by overheard him, and said, "How loudly that old woman snores! I must see if anything is the matter."

So he went into the cottage; and when he came to the bed, he saw the Wolf sleeping in it. "What! are you here, you old rascal? I have been looking for you," exclaimed he; and taking up his gun, he shot the old Wolf through the head.

But it is also said that the story ends in a different manner; for that one day, when Red-Cap was taking some presents to her grandmother, a Wolf met her, and wanted to mislead her; but she went straight on, and told her grandmother that she had met a Wolf, who said good-day, and who looked so hungrily out of his great eyes, as if he would have eaten her up had she not been on the high-road.

So her grandmother said, "We will shut the door, and then he cannot get in." Soon after, up came the Wolf, who tapped, and exclaimed, "I am Little Red-Cap, grandmother; I have some roast meat for you." But they kept quite quiet, and did not open the door; so the Wolf, after looking several times round the house, at last jumped on the roof, thinking to wait till Red-Cap went home in the evening, and then to creep after her and eat her in the darkness. The old woman, however, saw what the villain intended. There stood before the door a large stone trough, and she said to Little Red-Cap, "Take this bucket, dear: yesterday I boiled some meat in this water, now pour it into the stone trough." Then the

Wolf sniffed the smell of the meat, and his mouth watered, and he wished very much to taste   At last he stretched his neck too far over, so that he lost his balance, and fell down from the roof, right into the great trough below, and there he was drowned.

RUMPELSTILTSKIN

IN a certain kingdom once lived a poor miller who had a very beautiful daughter. She was moreover exceedingly shrewd and clever; and the miller was so vain and proud of her, that he one day told the king of the land that his daughter could spin gold out of straw. Now this king was very fond of money, and when he heard the miller's boast, his avarice was excited, and he ordered the girl to be brought before him. Then he led her to a chamber where there was a great quantity of straw, gave her a spinning wheel, and said, "All this must be spun into gold before morning, as you value your life." It was in vain that the poor maiden declared that she could do no such thing; the chamber was locked, and she remained alone.

She sat down in one corner of the room and began to lament over her sad fate, when on a sudden the door opened, and a droll-looking little man hobbled in, and said, " Good morrow to you, my good lass; what are you weeping for?" "Alas!" answered she, "I must spin this straw into gold, and I know not how." "What will you give me," said the little man, "to do it for you?" "My necklace," replied the maiden. He took her at her word, and set himself down to the wheel; round about it went merrily, and presently the work was done and the gold all spun.

When the king came and saw this, he was greatly astonished and pleased; but his heart grew still more greedy of gain, and he shut up the poor miller's daughter again with a fresh task. Then she knew not what to do, and sat down once more to weep; but the little man presently opened the door, and said, "What will you give me to do your task?" "The ring on my finger," replied she. So her little friend took the ring, and began to work at the wheel, till by morning all was finished again.

The king was vastly delighted to see all this glittering treasure; but still he was not satisfied, and took the miller's daughter into a yet larger room, and said, "All this must be spun to-night; and if you succeed, you shall be my queen." As soon as she was alone the dwarf came in, and said, "What will you give me to spin gold for you this third time?" "I have nothing left," said she. "Then promise me," said the little man, "your first little child when you are queen." "That may never be," thought the miller's daughter; and as she knew no other way to get her task done, she promised him what he asked, and he spun once more the whole heap of gold. The king came in the morning, and finding all he wanted, married her, and so the miller's daughter really became queen.

At the birth of her first little child the queen rejoiced very much, and forgot the little man and her promise; but one day he came into her chamber and reminded her of it. Then she grieved sorely at her misfortune, and offered him all the treasures of the kingdom in exchange; but in vain, till at last her tears softened him, and he said, "I will give you three days' grace, and if during that time you tell me my name, you shall keep your child."

Now the queen lay awake all night, thinking of all the odd names that she had ever heard, and dispatched messengers all over the land to enquire after new ones. The next day the little man came, and she began with Timothy, Benjamin, Jeremiah, and all the names she could remember; but to all of them he said, "That's not my name."

The second day she began with all the comical names she could hear of—Bandy-legs, Hunch-back, Crook-shanks, and so on, but the little gentleman still said to every one of them, "That's not my name."

The third day came back one of the messengers, and said, "I can hear of no one other name: but yesterday, as I was climbing a high hill among the trees of the forest where the fox and the hare bid each other good night, I saw a little hut, and before the hut burnt a fire, and round about the fire danced a funny little man upon one leg, and sang—

"'Merrily the feast I'll make,
To-day I'll brew, to-morrow bake;
Merrily I'll dance and sing,
For next day will a stranger bring:
Little does my lady dream
Rumpel-Stilts-Kin is my name.'"

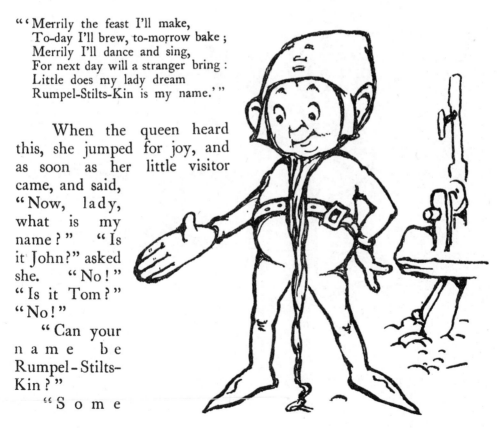

When the queen heard this, she jumped for joy, and as soon as her little visitor came, and said, "Now, lady, what is my name?" "Is it John?" asked she. "No!" "Is it Tom?" "No!"

"Can your name be Rumpel-Stilts-Kin?"

"Some

witch told you that! Some witch told you that!" cried the little man, and dashed his right foot in a rage so deep into the floor, that he was forced to lay hold of it with both hands to pull it out. Then he made the best of his way off, while everybody laughed at him for having had all his trouble for nothing.

THE
VALIANT
LITTLE TAILOR

ONE fine day a Tailor was sitting on his bench by the window in very high spirits, sewing away most diligently, and presently up the street came a country woman, crying, "Good jams for sale! Good jams for sale!" This cry sounded nice in the Tailor's ears, and, poking his diminutive head out of the window, he called out, "Here, my good woman, just bring your jams here!" The woman mounted the three steps up to the Tailor's house with her large basket, and began to open all the pots together before him. He looked at them all, held them up to the light, smelt them, and at last said, "These jams seem to me to be very nice, so you may weigh me out two ounces, my good woman; I don't object even if you make it a quarter of a pound." The woman, who hoped to have met with a good customer, gave

him all he wished, and went off grumbling, and in a very bad temper.

"Now!" exclaimed the Tailor, "Heaven will send me a blessing on this jam, and give me fresh strength and vigour;" and, taking the bread from the cupboard, he cut himself a slice the size of the whole loaf, and spread the jam upon it. "That will taste very nice," said he; "but, before I take a bite, I will just finish this waistcoat." So he put the bread on the table and stitched away, making larger and larger stitches every time for joy. Meanwhile the smell of the jam rose to the ceiling, where many flies were sitting, and enticed them down, so that soon a great swarm of them had pitched on the bread. "Holloa! who asked you?" exclaimed the Tailor, driving away the uninvited visitors; but the flies, not understanding his words, would not be driven off, and came back in greater numbers than before. This put the little man in a great passion, and, snatching up in his anger a bag of cloth, he brought it down with a merciless swoop upon them. When he raised it again he counted as many as seven lying dead before him with outstretched legs. "What a fellow you are!" said he to himself, astonished at his own bravery. "The whole town must hear of this." In great haste he cut himself out a band, hemmed it, and then put on it in large letters, "Seven at one Blow!" "Ah," said he, "not one city alone, the whole world shall hear it!" and his heart danced with joy, like a puppy-dog's tail.

The little Tailor bound the belt around his body, and made ready to travel forth into the wide world, feeling the workshop too small for his great deeds. Before he set out, however, he looked about his house to see if there were anything he could carry with him, but he found only an old cheese, which he pocketed, and observing a bird which was caught in the bushes before the door, he captured it, and put that in his pocket also. Soon after he set out boldly on his travels; and, as he was light and active, he felt no fatigue. His road led him up a hill, and when he arrived at the highest point of it he found a great Giant sitting there, who was gazing about him very composedly.

But the little Tailor went boldly up, and said, "Good day,

THE FROG PRINCE

LITTLE SNOW-WHITE

friend; truly you sit there and see the whole world stretched below you. I also am on my way thither to seek my fortune. Are you willing to go with me?"

The Giant looked with scorn at the little Tailor, and said, "You rascal! you wretched creature!"

"Perhaps so," replied the Tailor; "but here may be seen what sort of a man I am;" and, unbuttoning his coat, he showed the Giant his belt. The Giant read, "SEVEN AT ONE BLOW;" and supposing they were men whom the Tailor had killed, he felt some respect for him. Still he meant to try him first; so taking up a pebble, he squeezed it so hard that water dropped out of it. "Do as well as that," said he to the other, "if you have the strength."

"If it be nothing harder than that," said the Tailor, "that's child's play." And, diving into his pocket, he pulled out the cheese, and squeezed it till the whey ran out of it, and said, "Now, I fancy that I have done better than you."

The Giant wondered what to say, and could not believe it of the little man; so, catching up another pebble, he flung it so high that it almost went out of sight, saying, "There, you pigmy, do that if you can."

"Well done," said the Tailor; "but your pebble will fall down again to the ground. I will throw one up which will not come down;" and, dipping into his pocket, he took out the bird and threw it into the air. The bird, glad to be free, flew straight up, and then far away, and did not come back. "How does that little performance please you, friend?" asked the Tailor.

"You can throw well," replied the Giant; "now truly we will see if you are able to carry something uncommon." So saying, he took him to a large oak tree, which lay upon the ground, and said, "If you are strong enough, now help me to carry this tree out of the forest."

"With pleasure," replied the Tailor; "you may hold the trunk upon your shoulder, and I will lift the boughs and branches, they are the heaviest, and carry them."

The Giant took the trunk upon his shoulder, but the Tailor sat down on the branch, and the Giant, who could not look round, was compelled to carry the whole tree and the Tailor also. He being behind, was very cheerful, and laughed at the trick, and presently began to sing the song, " There rode three tailors out at the gate," as if the carrying of trees were a trifle. The Giant, after he had staggered a very short distance with his heavy load, could go no further, and called out, " Do you hear? I must drop the tree." The Tailor, jumping down, quickly embraced the tree with both arms, as if he had been carrying it, and said to the Giant, " Are you such a big fellow, and yet cannot you carry a tree by yourself?"

Then they travelled on further, and as they came to a cherry-tree, the Giant seized the top of the tree where the ripest cherries hung, and, bending it down, gave it to the Tailor to hold, telling him to eat. But the Tailor was far too weak to hold the tree down, and when the Giant let go, the tree flew up into the air, and the Tailor was taken with it. He came down on the other side, how-ever, unhurt, and the Giant said, " What does that mean? Are you not strong enough to hold that twig?" " My strength did not fail me," said the Tailor; " do you imagine that that was a hard task for one who has slain seven at one blow? I sprang over the tree simply because the hunters were shooting down here in the thicket. Jump after me if you can." The Giant made the attempt, but could not clear the tree, and stuck fast in the branches : so that in this affair, too, the Tailor had the advantage.

Then the Giant said, " Since you are such a brave fellow, come with me to my house, and stop a night with me." The Tailor agreed, and followed him; and when they came to the cave, there sat by the fire two other Giants, each with a roast sheep in his hand, of which he was eating. The Tailor sat down thinking. " Ah, this is very much more like the world than is my workshop." And soon the Giant pointed out·a bed where he could lie down and go to sleep. The bed, however, was too large for him, so he crept out of it, and lay down in a corner. When midnight came, and the Giant fancied the Tailor would be in a sound sleep, he got up, and taking a heavy iron bar, beat the bed right through at one stroke, and believed he had thereby given the Tailor his death blow. At the dawn of day the Giants went out into the forest, quite forgetting

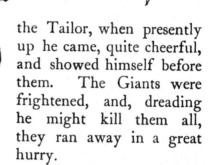

the Tailor, when presently
up he came, quite cheerful,
and showed himself before
them. The Giants were
frightened, and, dreading
he might kill them all,
they ran away in a great
hurry.

The Tailor travelled
on, always following his
nose, and after he had journeyed some long distance, he came into the courtyard of a royal
palace; and feeling very tired he laid himself
down on the ground and went to sleep. Whilst he lay there the
people came and viewed him on all sides, and read upon his belt,
"Seven at one blow." "Ah," they said, "what does this great
warrior here in time of peace? This must be some valiant hero."
So they went and told the King, knowing that, should war break
out, here was a valuable and useful man, whom one ought not to
part with at any price. The King took advice, and sent one of his
courtiers to the Tailor to beg for his fighting services, if he should
be awake. The messenger stopped at the sleeper's side, and waited
till he stretched out his limbs and unclosed his eyes, and then he
mentioned to him his message. "Solely for that reason did I come
here," was his answer; "I am quite willing to enter into the
King's service." Then he was taken away with great honour, and
a fine house was appointed him to dwell in.

The courtiers, however, became jealous of the Tailor, and

wished him at the other end of the world. "What will happen?" said they to one another. "If we go to war with him, when he strikes out seven will fall at one stroke, and nothing will be left for us to do." In their anger they came to the determination to resign, and they went altogether to the King, and asked his permission, saying, "We are not prepared to keep company with a man who kills seven at one blow." The King was sorry to lose all his devoted servants for the sake of one, and wished that he had never seen the Tailor, and would gladly have now been rid of him. He dared not, however, dismiss him, because he feared the Tailor might kill him and all his subjects, and seat himself upon the throne. For a long time he deliberated, till finally he came to a decision; and, sending for the Tailor, he told him that, seeing he was so great a hero, he wished to beg a favour of him. "In a certain forest in my kingdom," said the King, "there are two Giants, who, by murder, rapine, fire, and robbery, have committed great damage, and no one approaches them without endangering his own life. If you overcome and slay both these Giants, I will give you my only daughter in marriage, and the half of my kingdom for a dowry: a hundred knights shall accompany you, too, in order to render you assistance."

"Ah, that is something for a man like me," thought the Tailor to himself: "a lovely Princess and half a kingdom are not offered to one every day." "Oh, yes," he replied, "I will soon settle these two Giants, and a hundred horsemen are not needed for that purpose; he who kills seven at one blow has no fear of two."

Speaking thus, the little Tailor set out, followed by the hundred knights, to whom he said, immediately they came to the edge of the forest, "You must stay here; I prefer to meet these Giants alone."

Then he ran off into the forest, peering about him on all sides; and after a while he saw the two Giants sound asleep under a tree, snoring so loudly that the branches above them shook violently. The Tailor, bold as a lion, filled both his pockets with stones and climbed up the tree. When he got to the middle of it he crawled along a bough, so that he sat just above the sleepers, and then he let fall one stone after another upon the body of one of them. For some time the Giant did not move, until, at last awaking, he pushed his companion, and said, " Why are you hitting me ? "

" You have been dreaming," he answered ; " I did not touch you." So they laid themselves down again to sleep, and presently the Tailor threw a stone down upon the other. " What is that ? " he cried. " Why are you knocking me about ? "

" I did not touch you ; you are dreaming," said the first. So they argued for a few minutes ; but, both being very weary with the day's work, they soon went to sleep again. Then the Tailor began his fun again, and, picking out the largest stone, threw it with all his strength upon the chest of the first Giant. " This is too bad ! " he exclaimed ; and, jumping up like a madman, he fell upon his companion, who considered himself equally injured, and they set to in such good earnest, that they rooted up trees and beat one another about until they both fell dead upon the ground. Then the Tailor jumped down, saying, " What a piece of luck they did not pull up the tree on which I sat, or else I must have jumped on another like a squirrel, for I am not used to flying." Then he drew his sword, and, cutting a deep wound in the breast of both, he went to the horsemen and said, " The deed is done ; I have given each his death-stroke ; but it was a tough job, for in their defence they uprooted trees to protect themselves with ; still, all that is of no use when such an one as I come, who slew seven at one stroke."

" And are you not wounded ? " they asked.

" How can you ask me that ? they have not injured a hair of my head," replied the little man. The knights could hardly believe him, till, riding into the forest, they found the Giants lying dead, and the uprooted trees around them.

Then the Tailor demanded the promised reward of the King ; but he repented of his promise, and began to think of some new plan to shake off the hero. " Before you receive my daughter and the half of my kingdom," said he to him, " you must execute another brave deed. In the forest there lives a unicorn that commits great damage, you must first catch him."

" I fear a unicorn less than I did two Giants ! Seven at one blow is my motto," said the Tailor. So he carried with him a rope and an axe and went off to the forest, ordering those, who were told to accompany him, to wait on the outskirts. He had not to hunt long, for soon the unicorn approached, and prepared to rush at him as if it would pierce him on the spot. "Steady! steady!" he exclaimed, "that is not done so easily;" and, waiting till the animal was close upon him, he sprang nimbly behind a tree. The unicorn, rushing with all its force against the tree, stuck its horn so fast in the trunk that it could not pull it out again, and so it remained prisoner.

"Now I have got him," said the Tailor; and, coming from behind the tree, he first bound the rope around its neck, and then cutting the horn out of the tree with his axe, he arranged everything, and, leading the unicorn, brought it before the King.

The King, however, would not yet deliver over the promised reward, and made a third demand, that, before the marriage, the Tailor should capture a wild boar which did much damage, and he should have the huntsmen to help him. "With pleasure," was the reply; "it is a mere nothing." The huntsmen, however, he left behind, to their great joy, for this wild boar had already so often

hunted them, that they saw no fun in now hunting it. As soon as the boar perceived the Tailor, it ran at him with gaping mouth and glistening teeth, and tried to throw him down on the ground; but our flying hero sprang into a little chapel which stood near, and out again at a window, on the other side, in a moment. The boar ran after him, but he, skipping around, closed the door behind it, and there the furious beast was caught, for it was much too unwieldy and heavy to jump out of the window.

The Tailor now ordered the huntsmen up, that they might see his prisoner with their own eyes; but our hero presented himself before the King, who was obliged at last, whether he would or no, to keep his word, and surrender his daughter and the half of his kingdom.

If he had known that it was no warrior, but only a Tailor, who stood before him, it would have grieved him still more.

So the wedding was celebrated with great magnificence, though with little rejoicing, and out of a Tailor there was made a King.

A short time afterwards the young Queen heard her husband talking in his sleep, and saying, "Boy, make me a coat, and then stitch up these trowsers, or I will lay the yard-measure over your shoulders!" Then she understood of what condition her husband was, and complained in the morning to her father, and begged he would free her from her husband, who was nothing more than a tailor. The King comforted her by saying, "This night leave your chamber-door open; my servants shall stand outside, and when he is asleep they shall come in, bind him, and carry him away to a ship, which shall take him out into the wide world." The wife was pleased with the proposal; but the King's armour-bearer, who had overheard all, went to the young King and revealed the whole plot. "I will soon put an end to this affair," said the valiant little Tailor. In the evening at their usual time they went to bed, and when his wife thought he slept she got up, opened the door, and laid herself down again.

The Tailor, however, only pretended to be asleep, and began to call out in a loud voice, "Boy, make me a coat, and then stitch up these trowsers, or I will lay the yard-measure about your shoulders! Seven have I slain with one blow, two Giants have I killed, a unicorn have I led captive, and a wild boar have I caught, and shall I be afraid of those who stand outside my room?"

When the men heard these words spoken by the Tailor, a great fear came over them, and they ran away as if wild huntsmen were following them; neither afterwards dared any man venture to oppose him. Thus the Tailor became a King, and so he lived for the rest of his life.

THE SIX SWANS

A KING was once hunting in a large wood, and pursued his game so hotly that none of his courtiers could follow him. But when evening approached he stopped, and looking around him perceived that he had lost himself. He sought a path out of the forest but could not find one, and presently he saw an old woman, with a nodding head, who came up to him. "My good woman," said he to her, "can you not show me the way out of the forest?" "Oh, yes, my lord King," she replied; "I can do that very well, but upon one condition, which if you do not fulfil, you will never again get out of the wood, but will die of hunger."

"What, then, is this condition?" asked the King.

"I have a daughter," said the old woman, "who is as beautiful as any one you can find in the whole world, and well deserves to be your bride. Now, if you will make her your Queen, I will show you your way out of the wood." In the anxiety of his heart, the King consented, and the old woman led him to her cottage, where the daughter was sitting by the fire. She received the King as if she had expected him, and he saw at once that she was very beautiful, but yet she did not quite please him, for he could not look at her without a secret shuddering. However, he took the maiden upon his horse, and the old woman showed him the way, and the King arrived safely at his palace, where the wedding was to be celebrated.

The King had
been married once
before, and had
seven children by
his first wife, six
boys and a girl,
whom he loved
above everything
else in the world.
He became afraid,
soon, that the step-
mother might not
treat his children
very well, and
might even do
them some great
injury, so he took
them away to a
lonely castle which
stood in the midst of a forest. The castle
was so entirely hidden, and the way to
it was so difficult to discover, that he
himself could not have found it if a wise
woman had not. given him a ball of cotton
which had the wonderful property, when
he threw it before him, of unrolling itself
and showing him the right path. The
King went, however, so often to see his
dear children, that the Queen, noticing his absence, became inquisitive, and wished to know what he went to fetch out of the forest.
So she gave his servants a great quantity of money, and they dis-
closed to her the secret, and also told her of the ball of cotton
which alone could show her the way. She had now no peace until
she discovered where this ball was concealed, and then she made
some fine silken shirts, and, as she had learnt of her mother, she
sewed within each a charm. One day soon after, when the King

was gone out hunting, she took the little shirts and went into the forest, and the cotton showed her the path. The children, seeing some one coming in the distance, thought it was their dear father, and ran out full of joy. Then she threw over each of them a shirt, that, as it touched their bodies, changed them into Swans which flew away over the forest. The Queen then went home quite contented, and thought she was free of her step-children; but the little girl had not met her with the brothers, and the Queen did not know of her.

The following day the King went to visit his children, but he found only the Maiden. "Where are your brothers?" asked he. "Ah, dear father," she replied, "they are gone away and have left me alone;" and she told him how she had looked out of the window and seen them changed into Swans, which had flown over the forest; and then she showed him the feathers which they had dropped in the courtyard, and which she had collected together. The King was much grieved, but he did not think that his wife could have done this wicked deed, and, as he feared the girl might also be stolen away, he took her with him. She was, however, so much afraid of the stepmother, that she begged him not to stop more than one night in the castle.

The poor Maiden thought to herself, "This is no longer my place; I will go and seek my brothers;" and when night came she escaped and went quite deep into the wood. She walked all night long, and a great part of the next day, until she could go no further from weariness. Just then she saw a rough-looking hut, and going in, she found a room with six little beds, but she dared not get into one, so crept under, and laying herself upon the hard earth, prepared to pass the night there. Just as the sun was setting, she heard a rustling, and saw six white Swans come flying in at the window. They settled on the ground and began blowing one another until they had blown all their feathers off, and their swan's down slipped from them like a shirt. Then the Maiden knew them at once for her brothers, and gladly crept out from under the bed, and the brothers were not less glad to see their sister, but their joy was of short duration. "Here you must not stay," said they to her; "this is a robbers' hiding-place; if they should return and find you here, they would murder you." "Can you not protect me, then?" enquired the sister.

"No," they replied; "for we can only lay aside our swan's feathers for a quarter of an hour each evening, and for that time we regain our human form, but afterwards we resume our changed appearance."

Their sister then asked them, with tears, "Can you not be restored again?"

"Oh, no," replied they; "the conditions are too difficult. For six long years you must neither speak nor laugh, and during that time you must sew together for us six little shirts of star-flowers, and should there fall a single word from your lips, then all your labour will be in vain." Just as the brothers finished speaking, the quarter of an hour elapsed, and they all flew out of the window again like Swans.

The little sister, however, made a solemn resolution to rescue her brothers, or die in the attempt; and she left the cottage, and, penetrating deep into the forest, passed the night amid the branches of a tree. The next morning she went out and collected the star-flowers to sew together. She had no one to converse with, and for laughing she had no spirits, so there up in the tree she sat, intent upon her work.

After she had passed some time there, it happened that the King of that country was hunting in the forest, and his huntsmen came beneath the tree on which the Maiden sat. They called to her and asked, "Who art thou?" But she gave no answer. "Come down to us," continued they; "we will do thee no harm." She simply shook her head, and, when they pressed her further with questions, she threw down to them her gold necklace, hoping therewith to satisfy them. They did not, however, leave her, and she threw down her girdle, but in vain! and even her rich dress did not make them desist. At last the huntsman himself climbed the tree and brought down the Maiden, and took her before the King.

The King asked her, "Who art thou? What dost thou upon

that tree?" But she did not answer; and then he questioned her in all the languages that he knew, but she remained dumb to all, as a fish. Since, however, she was so beautiful, the King's heart was touched, and he conceived for her a strong affection. Then he put around her his cloak, and, placing her before him on his horse, took her to his castle. There he ordered rich clothing to be made for her, and, although her beauty shone as the sunbeams, not a word escaped her. The King placed her by his side at table, and there her dignified mien and manners so won upon him, that he said, "This Maiden will I marry, and no other in the world;" and after some days he wedded her.

Now, the King had a wicked stepmother, who was discontented with his marriage, and spoke evil of the young Queen. "Who knows whence the wench comes?" said she. "She who cannot speak is not worthy of a King." A year after, when the Queen brought her first-born into the world, the old woman took him away. Then she went to the King and complained that the Queen was a murderess. The King, however, would not believe it, and suffered no one to do any injury to his wife, who sat composedly sewing at her shirts and paying attention to nothing else. When a second child was born, the false stepmother used the same deceit, but the King again would not listen to her words, saying, "She is too pious and good to act so: could she but speak

and defend herself, her innocence would come to light." But when again, the old woman stole away the third child, and then accused the Queen, who answered not a word to the accusation, the King was obliged to give her up to be tried, and she was condemned to suffer death by fire.

When the time had elapsed, and the sentence was to be carried out, it happened that the very day had come round when her dear brothers should be set free; the six shirts were also ready, all but the last, which yet wanted the left sleeve. As she was led to the scaffold, she placed the shirts upon her arm, and just as she had mounted it, and the fire was about to be kindled, she looked around, and saw six Swans come flying through the air. Her heart leapt for joy as she perceived her deliverers approaching, and soon the Swans, flying towards her, alighted so near that she was enabled to throw over them the shirts, and as soon as she had so done, their feathers fell off and the brothers stood up alive and well; but the youngest was without his left arm, instead of which he had a swan's wing. They embraced and kissed each other, and the Queen, going to the King, who was thunderstruck, began to say, " Now may I speak, my dear husband, and prove to you that I am innocent and falsely accused; " and then she told him how the wicked woman had stolen away and hidden her three children. When she had concluded, the King was overcome with joy, and the wicked stepmother was led to the scaffold and bound to the stake and burnt to ashes.

The King and Queen for ever after lived in peace and prosperity with their six brothers.

THE FROG PRINCE

IN the olden time, when wishing was having, there lived a King, whose daughters were all beautiful; but the youngest was so exceedingly beautiful that the Sun himself, although he saw her very, very often, was delighted every time she came out into the sunshine.

Near the castle of this King was a large and gloomy forest, where in the midst stood an old lime-tree, beneath whose branches splashed a little fountain; so, whenever it was very hot, the King's youngest daughter ran off into this wood, and sat down by the side of the fountain; and, when she felt dull, would often divert herself by throwing a golden ball up into the air and catching it again. And this was her favourite amusement.

Now, one day it happened that this golden ball, when the King's daughter threw it into the air, did not fall down into her hand, but on to the grass; and then it rolled right into the fountain. The King's daughter followed the ball with her eyes, but it disappeared beneath the water, which was so deep that she could not see to the bottom. Then she began to lament, and to cry more loudly and more loudly; and, as she cried, a voice called out, "Why weepest thou, O King's daughter? thy tears would melt even a stone to pity." She looked around to the spot whence the voice came, and saw a Frog stretching his thick, ugly head out of the water. "Ah! you old water-paddler," said she, "was it you that spoke? I am weeping for my golden ball which bounced away from me into the water."

"Be quiet, and do not cry," replied the Frog; "I can give thee good assistance. But what wilt thou give me if I succeed in fetching thy plaything up again?"

"What would you like, dear Frog?" said she "My dresses, my pearls and jewels, or the golden crown which I wear?"

The Frog replied, "Dresses, or jewels, or golden crowns, are not for me; but if thou wilt love me, and let me be thy companion and playmate, and sit at thy table, and eat from thy little golden plate, and drink out of thy cup, and sleep in thy little bed,—if thou wilt promise me all these things, then I will dive down and fetch up thy golden ball."

"Oh, I will promise you all," said she, "if you will only get me my golden ball." But she thought to herself, "What is the silly Frog chattering about? Let him stay in the water with his equals; he cannot enter into society." Then the Frog, as soon as he had received her promise, drew his head under the water and dived down. Presently he swam up again with the golden ball in his mouth, and threw it on to the grass. The King's daughter was full of joy when she again saw her beautiful plaything; and, taking it up, she ran off immediately. "Stop! stop!" cried the Frog; "take me with thee. I cannot run as thou canst."

But this croaking was of no avail; although it was loud enough, the King's daughter did not hear it, but, hastening home, soon forgot the poor Frog, who was obliged to leap back into the fountain.

The next day, when the King's daughter was sitting at table with her father and all his courtiers, and was eating from her own little golden plate, something was heard coming up the marble stairs, splish-splash, splish-splash; and when it arrived at the top, it knocked at the door, and a voice said—

"Open the door, thou youngest daughter of the King!"

So she arose and went to see who it was that called to her; but when she opened the door and caught sight of the Frog, she shut it again very quickly and with great passion, and sat down at the table, looking exceedingly pale.

But the King perceived that her heart was beating violently, and asked her whether it were a giant who had come to fetch her away who stood at the door. "Oh, no!" answered she; "it is no giant, but an ugly Frog."

"What does the Frog want with you?" said the King.

"Oh, dear father, yesterday when I was playing by the fountain, my golden ball fell into the water, and this Frog fetched it up again because I cried so much: but first, I must tell you, he pressed me so much, that I promised him he should be my companion. I never thought that he could come out of the water, but somehow he has managed to jump out, and now he wants to come in here."

At that moment there was another knock, and a voice said,—

> "King's daughter, youngest,
>   Open the door.
> Hast thou forgotten
>   Thy promises made
> At the fountain so clear
>   'Neath the lime-tree's shade?
> King's daughter, youngest,
>   Open the door."

Then the King said, "What you have promised, that you must perform; go and let him in." So the King's daughter went and opened the door, and the Frog hopped in after her right up to her chair: and as soon as she was seated, he said, "Lift me up;" but she hesitated so long that the King had to order her to obey. And as soon as the Frog sat on the chair he jumped on to the table and said, "Now push thy plate near me, that we may eat together." And she did so, but as every one noticed, very unwillingly. The Frog seemed to relish his dinner very much, but every bit that the King's daughter ate nearly choked her, till at last the Frog said, "I

have satisfied my hunger, and feel very tired; wilt thou carry me
upstairs now into thy chamber, and make thy bed ready that we
may sleep together?" At this speech the King's daughter began
to cry, for she was afraid of the cold Frog, and dared not touch
him; and besides, he actually wanted to sleep in her own beautiful,
clean bed!

But her tears only made the King very angry, and he said,
" He who helped you in the time of your trouble must not now be
despised!" So she took the Frog up with two fingers, and put
him into a corner of her chamber. But as she lay in her bed, he

crept up to it, and said,
" I am so very tired
that I shall sleep well;
do take me up, or I
will tell thy father."
This speech put the
King's daughter into a
terrible passion, and
catching the Frog up,
she threw him with all
her strength against the
wall, saying,
" Now will
you be quiet,
y o u u g l y
Frog!"

But as
h e f e l l h e
was changed
from a frog
into a hand-
some Prince
with beauti-
ful eyes, who
after a little
while became

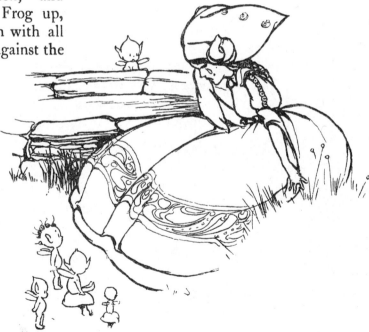

her dear companion and betrothed. Then he told her how he had been transformed by an evil witch, and that no one but herself could have had the power to take him out of the fountain; and that on the morrow they would go together into his own kingdom.

The next morning, as soon as the sun rose, a carriage drawn by eight white horses, with ostrich feathers on their heads, and golden bridles, drove up to the door of the palace, and behind the carriage stood the trusty Henry, the servant of the young Prince. When his master was changed into a frog, trusty Henry had grieved so much that he had bound three iron bands around his heart, for fear it should break with grief and sorrow.

But now that the carriage was ready to carry the young Prince to his own country, the faithful Henry (who was also the trusty Henry) helped in the bride and bridegroom, and placed himself in the seat behind, full of joy at his master's release. They had not proceeded far when the Prince heard a crack as if something had broken behind the carriage; so he put his head out of the window and asked trusty Henry what was broken, and faithful Henry answered, " It was not the carriage, my master, but an iron band which I bound around my heart when it was in such grief because you were changed into a frog."

Twice afterwards on the journey there was the same noise, and each time the Prince thought

that it was some part of the carriage that had given way; but it was only the breaking of the bands which bound the heart of the trusty Henry (who was also the faithful Henry), and who was thenceforward free and happy.

LITTLE SNOW-WHITE

IT was in the middle of winter, when the broad flakes of snow were falling around, that a certain queen sat working at her window, the frame of which was made of fine black ebony; and, as she was looking out upon the snow, she pricked her finger, and three drops of blood fell upon it. Then she gazed thoughtfully down on the red drops which sprinkled the white snow and said, " Would that my little daughter may be as white as that snow, as red as the blood, and as black as the ebony window-frame ! " And so the little girl grew up; her skin was as white as snow, her cheeks as rosy as blood, and her hair as black as ebony; and she was called Snow-White.

But this queen died; and the king soon married another wife, who was very beautiful, but so proud that she could not bear to think that any one could surpass her. She had a magical looking-glass, to which she used to go and gaze upon herself in it, and say,

> " Tell me, glass, tell me true !
> Of all the ladies in the land,
> Who is fairest ? tell me who ? "

And the glass answered, " Thou, Queen, art fairest in the land."

But Snow-White grew more and more beautiful; and when she was seven years old, she was as bright as the day, and fairer than the queen herself. Then the glass one day answered the queen, when she went to consult it as usual:

> "Thou, Queen, may'st fair and beauteous be,
> But Snow-White is lovelier far than thee?"

When the queen heard this she turned pale with rage and envy; and calling to one of her servants said, "Take Snow-White away into the wide wood, that I may never see her more." Then the servant led the little girl away; but his heart melted when she begged him to spare her life, and he said, "I will not hurt thee, thou pretty child." So he left her there alone; and though he thought it most likely that the wild beasts would tear her to pieces, he felt as if a great weight were taken off his heart when he had made up his mind not to kill her, but leave her to her fate.

Then poor Snow-White wandered along through the wood in great fear; and the wild beasts roared around, but none did her any harm. In the evening she came to a little cottage, and went in there to rest, for her little feet would carry her no further. Everything was spruce and neat in the cottage: on the table was spread a white cloth, and there were seven little plates with seven little loaves and seven little glasses with wine in them; and knives and forks laid in order, and by the wall stood seven little beds. Then, as she was exceedingly hungry, she picked a little piece off each loaf, and drank a very little wine out of each glass; and after that she thought she would lie down and rest. So she tried all the little beds; and one was too long, and another was too short, till, at last, the seventh suited her; and there she laid herself down and went to sleep. Presently in came the masters of the cottage, who were seven little dwarfs that lived among the mountains, and dug and searched about for gold. They lighted up their seven lamps, and saw directly that all was not right. The first said, "Who has been sitting on my stool?" The second, "Who has been eating off my plate?" The third, "Who has been picking at my bread?" The fourth, "Who has been meddling with my spoon?" The fifth "Who has been handling,

my fork?" The sixth, "Who has been cutting with my knife?" The seventh, "Who has been drinking my wine?" Then the first looked around and said, "Who has been lying on my bed?" And the rest came running to him, and every one cried out that somebody had been upon his bed. But the seventh saw Snow-White, and called upon his brethren to come and look at her; and they cried out with wonder and astonishment, and brought their lamps and gazing upon her, they said, "Good heavens! what a lovely child she is!" And they were delighted to see her, and took care not to waken her; and the seventh dwarf slept an hour with each of the other dwarfs in turn, till the night was gone.

In the morning Snow-White told them all her story; and they pitied her, and said if she would keep all things in order, and cook and wash, and knit and spin for them, she might stay where she was, and they would take good care of her. Then they went out all day long to their work, seeking for gold and silver in the mountains; and Snow-White remained at home; and they warned her, saying, "The queen will soon find out where you are, so take care and let no one in."

But the queen, now that she thought Snow-White was dead, believed that she was certainly the handsomest lady in the land; so she went to her glass and said;

"Tell me, glass, tell me true!
Of all the ladies in the land,
Who is fairest? tell me who?"

And the glass answered,

> "Thou, Queen, thou art fairest in all this land,
> But over the hills, in the greenwood shade,
> Where the seven dwarfs their dwelling have made,
> There Snow-White is hiding; and she
> Is lovelier far, Oh Queen, than thee."

Then the queen was very much alarmed; for she knew that the glass always spoke the truth, and was sure that the servant had betrayed her.   And as she could not bear to think that any one lived who was more beautiful than she was, she disguised herself as an old pedlar woman and went her way over the hills to the place where the dwarfs dwelt.   Then she knocked at the door, and cried, " Fine wares to sell ! "   Snow-White looked out of the window, and said, " Good-day, good woman; what have you to sell ? "   " Good wares, fine wares," replied she; " laces and bobbins of all colours."   " I will let the old lady in; she seems to be a very good sort of a body," thought Snow-White; so she ran down, and unbolted the door. " Bless me ! " said the woman, " how badly your stays are laced. Let me lace them up with one of my nice new laces."   Snow-White did not dream of any mischief; so she stood up before the old woman who set to work so nimbly, and pulled the lace so tightly that Snow-White lost her breath, and fell down as if she were dead.   " There's an end of all thy beauty," said the spiteful queen, and went away home.

In the evening the seven dwarfs returned; and I need not say how grieved they were to see their faithful Snow-White stretched upon the ground motionless, as if she were quite dead.   However, they lifted her up, and when they found what was the matter, they cut the lace; and in a little time she began to breathe, and soon came to herself again.   Then they said, " The old woman was the queen; take care another time, and let no one in when we are away."

When the queen got home, she went to her glass, and spoke to it, but to her surprise it replied in the same words as before.

Then the blood ran cold in her heart with spite and malice to hear that Snow-White still lived; and she dressed herself up again in a disguise, but very different from the one she wore before, and took

with her a poisoned comb.   When she reached the dwarfs' cottage,
she knocked at the door, and cried, " Fine wares to sell ! " but Snow-
White said, " I dare not let anyone in."   Then the queen said,
" Only look at my beautiful combs ; " and gave her the poisoned one.
And it looked so pretty that the little girl took it up and put it into
her hair to try it ; but the moment it touched her head the poison
was so powerful that she fell down senseless.   "There you may lie,"
said the queen, and went her way.   But by good luck the dwarfs
returned very early that evening ; and when they saw Snow-White
lying on the ground, they thought what had happened, and soon
found the poisoned comb.   And when they took it away, she
recovered, and told them all that had
passed ; and they warned her once more
not to open the door to anyone.

Meantime the queen went home to
her glass, and trembled with rage when
she received exactly the same answer as
before ; and she said, " Snow-White shall
die, if it costs me my life."   So she went
secretly into a chamber, and prepared a
poisoned apple : the outside looked very
rosy and tempting, but whosoever tasted
it was sure to die.   Then she dressed herself up as a peasant's wife, and travelled
over the hills to the dwarfs' cottage, and
knocked at the door ; but Snow-White
put her head out of the window, and
said, " I dare not let any one in, for the
dwarfs have told me not to."   " Do as
you please," said the old woman, " but
at any rate take this pretty apple ; I will
make you a present of it."   " No," said
Snow-White, " I dare not take it."
" You silly girl ! " answered the other,
" what are you afraid of ? do you think
it is poisoned ?   Come ! do you eat one

part, and I will eat the other." Now the apple was so prepared that one side was good, though the other side was poisoned. Then Snow-White was very much tempted to taste, for the apple looked exceedingly nice; and when she saw the old woman eat, she could refrain no longer. But she had scarcely put the piece into her mouth when she fell down dead upon the ground. "This time nothing will save thee," said the queen; and she went home to her glass, and at last it said,

"Thou, Queen, art the fairest of all the fair."

And then her envious heart was glad, and as happy as such a heart could be.

When evening came, and the dwarfs returned home, they found Snow-White lying on the ground; no breath passed her lips, and they were afraid that she was quite dead. They lifted her up, and combed her hair, and washed her face with wine and water; but all was in vain. So they laid her down upon a bier, and all seven watched and bewailed her three whole days; and then they proposed to bury her; but her cheeks were still rosy, and her face looked just as it did while she was alive; so they said, "We will never bury her in the cold ground." And they made a coffin of glass so that they might still look at her, and wrote her name upon it in golden letters, and that she was a king's daughter. Then the coffin was placed upon the hill, and one of the dwarfs always sat by it and watched. And the birds of the air came too, and bemoaned Snow-White. First of all came an owl, and then a raven, but at last came a dove.

And thus Snow-White lay for a long, long time, and still only looked as though she were asleep; for she was even now as white as snow, and as red as blood, and as black as ebony. At last a prince came and called at the dwarfs' house; and he saw Snow-White, and read what was written in golden letters. Then he offered the dwarfs money, and earnestly prayed them to let him take her away; but they said, "We will not part with her for all the gold in the world." At last, however, they had pity on him, and gave him the coffin; but the moment he lifted it up to carry it home with him, the piece of apple fell from between her lips, and Snow-White awoke, and exclaimed, "Where am I?" And the prince answered, "Thou art safe with me." Then he told her all that had happened, and said, "I love you better than all the world; come with me to my father's palace, and you shall be my wife." Snow-White consented, and went home with the prince; and everything was prepared with great pomp and splendour for their wedding.

To the feast was invited, among the rest, Snow-White's old enemy, the queen; and as she was dressing herself in fine, rich clothes, she looked in the glass and said, "Tell me, glass, tell me true! Of all the ladies in the land, Who is fairest? tell me who?" And the glass answered, "Thou, lady, art the loveliest *here*, I ween; But lovelier far is the new-made queen."

When she heard this, the queen started with rage; but her envy and curiosity were so great, that she could not help setting out to see the bride. And when she arrived, and saw that it was no other than Snow-White, whom she thought had been dead a long while, she choked with passion, and fell ill and died; but Snow-White and the prince lived and reigned happily over that land many, many years.

THE LITTLE BROTHER AND SISTER

THERE was once a little Brother who took his Sister by the hand, and said, " Since our own dear mother's death we have not had one happy hour; our stepmother beats us every day, and, when we come near her, kicks us away with her foot. Come, let us wander forth into the wide world." So all day long they travelled over meadows, fields, and stony roads. By the evening they came into a large forest, and laid themselves down in a hollow tree, and went to sleep. When they awoke the next morning, the sun had already risen high in the heavens, and its beams made the tree so hot that the little boy said to his sister, "I am so very thirsty, that if I knew where there was a brook, I would go and drink. Ah! I think I hear one running;" and so saying, he got up, and taking his Sister's hand they went to look for the brook.

The wicked stepmother, however, was a witch, and had witnessed the departure of the two children: so, sneaking after them secretly, as is the habit of witches, she had enchanted all the springs in the forest.

Presently they found a brook, which ran trippingly over the pebbles, and the Brother would have drunk out of it, but the Sister heard how it said as it ran along, "Who drinks of me will become a tiger!" So the Sister exclaimed, "I pray you, Brother, drink not, or you will become a tiger, and tear me to pieces!" So the Brother did not drink, although his thirst was very great, and he said, "I will wait till the next brook." As they came to the second, the Sister heard it say, "Who drinks of me becomes a wolf!" The Sister ran up crying, "Brother, do not, pray do not drink, or you will become a wolf and eat me up!" Then the Brother did not drink, saying, "I will wait until we come to the next spring, but then I must drink, you may say what you will; my thirst is much too great." Just as they reached the third brook, the Sister heard the voice saying, "Who drinks of me will become a fawn—who drinks of me will become a fawn!" So the Sister said, "Oh, my Brother! do not drink, or you will be changed into a fawn, and run away from me!" But he had already kneeled down, and he drank of the water, and, as the first drops passed his lips, his shape took that of a fawn.

At first the Sister wept over her little, changed Brother, and he wept too, and knelt by her, very sorrowful; but at last the maiden said, "Be still, dear little Fawn, and I will never forsake you?" and, taking off her golden garter, she placed it around his neck, and, weaving rushes, made a girdle to lead him with. This she tied to him, and taking the other end in her hand, she led him away, and they travelled deeper and deeper into the forest. After they had gone a long distance they came to a little hut, and the maiden, peeping in, found it empty, and thought, " Here we can stay and dwell." Then she looked for leaves and moss to make a soft couch for the Fawn, and every morning she went out and collected roots and berries and nuts for herself, and tender grass for the Fawn. In the evening when the Sister was tired, and had said her prayers, she laid her head upon the back of the Fawn, which served for a pillow, on which she slept soundly. Had but the Brother regained his own proper form, their lives would have been happy indeed.

Thus they dwelt in this wilderness, and some time had elapsed when it happened that the King of the country had a great hunt in the forest; and now sounded through the trees the blowing of horns, the barking of dogs, and the lusty cry of the hunters, so that the little Fawn heard them, and wanted very much to join in. " Ah ! " said he to his Sister, " let me go to the hunt, I cannot restrain myself any longer; " and he begged so hard that at last she consented. " But," she told him, " return again in the evening, for I shall shut my door against the wild huntsmen, and, that I may know you, do you knock, and say, ' Sister, dear, let me in,' and if you do not speak I shall not open the door." As soon as she had said this, the little Fawn sprang off quite glad and merry in the fresh breeze. The King and his huntsmen perceived the beautiful animal, and pursued him; but they could not catch him, and when they thought they certainly had him, he sprang away over the bushes, and got out of sight. Just as it was getting dark, he ran up to the hut, and, knocking, said, " Sister mine, let me in." Then she unfastened the little door, and he went in, and rested all night long upon his soft couch. The next morning the hunt was commenced again, and as soon as the little Fawn heard the horns and the tally-ho of the sportsmen he could not rest, and said, " Sister, dear, open the door; I must be off." The Sister opened it, saying, " Return at evening, mind, and say the words as before." When the King and his huntsmen saw him again, the Fawn with the golden necklace, they followed him close, but he was too nimble and quick for them. The whole day long they kept up with him, but towards evening the huntsmen made a circle around him, and one wounded him slightly in the hinder foot, so that he could run but slowly.

Then one of them slipped after him to the little hut, and heard him say, "Sister, dear, open the door," and saw that the door was opened and immediately shut behind him. The huntsman, having observed all this, went and told the King what he had seen and heard, and he said, "On the morrow I will pursue him once again."

The Sister, however, was terribly afraid when she saw that her Fawn was wounded, and, washing off the blood, she put herbs upon the foot, and said, "Go and rest upon your bed, dear Fawn, that your wound may heal." It was so slight, that the next morning he felt nothing of it, and when he heard the hunting cries outside, he exclaimed, "I cannot stop away—I must be there, and none shall catch me so easily again!" The Sister wept very much and told him, "Soon will they kill you, and I shall be here alone in this forest, forsaken by all the world: I cannot let you go."

"I shall die here in vexation," answered the Fawn, "if you do not, for

when I hear the horn, I think I shall jump out of my skin." The Sister, finding she could not prevent him, opened the door, with a heavy heart, and the Fawn jumped out, quite delighted, into the forest. As soon as the King perceived him, he said to his huntsmen, " Follow him all day long till the evening, but let no one do him any harm." Then when the sun had set, the King asked his huntsman to show him the hut ; and as they came to it he knocked at the door and said, " Let me in, dear Sister." Upon this the door opened, and, stepping in, the King saw a maiden more beautiful than he had ever beheld before. She was frightened when she saw, not her Fawn, but a man enter, who had a golden crown upon his head. But the King, looking at her with a kindly glance, held out to her his hand, saying, " Will you go with me to my castle, and be my dear wife ? " " Oh, yes," replied the maiden ; " but the Fawn must go too : him I will never forsake." The King replied, " He shall remain with you as long as you live, and shall never want."

The King took the beautiful maiden upon his horse, and rode to his castle, where the wedding was celebrated with great splendour, and she became Queen, and they lived together a long time ; while the Fawn was taken care of and played about the castle garden.

The wicked stepmother, however, on whose account the children had wandered forth into the world, had supposed that long ago the Sister had been torn into pieces by the wild beasts, and the little Brother in his Fawn's shape hunted to death by the hunters. As soon, therefore, as she heard how happy they had become, and how everything prospered with them, envy and jealousy were aroused in her wicked heart, and left her no peace ; and she was always thinking in what way she could bring misfortune upon them.

Her own daughter, who was as ugly as night, and had but one eye, for which she was continually reproached, said, " The luck of being a Queen has never happened to me." " Be quiet now," replied the old woman, " and make yourself contented : when the time comes I will help and assist you." As soon, then,

THE GOLDEN GOOSE

THE CHANGELING

as the time came when the Queen gave birth to a beautiful little
boy, which happened when the King was out hunting, the old
witch took the form of a chambermaid, and got into the room
where the Queen was lying, and said to her, "The bath is ready,
which will restore you and give you fresh strength ; be quick before
it gets cold." Her daughter being at hand, they carried the weak
Queen between them into the room, and laid her in the bath, and
then, shutting the door, they ran off; but first they made up an
immense fire in the stove, which must soon suffocate the poor young
Queen.

When this was done, the old woman took her daughter, and,
putting a cap upon her head, laid her in the bed in the Queen's place.
She gave her, too, the form and appearance of the real Queen, as far
as she was able; but she could not restore the lost eye, and, so that
the King might not notice it, she turned her upon that side where
there was no eye.

When midnight came, and every one was asleep, the nurse, who
sat by herself wide awake, near the cradle, in the nursery, saw the
door open and the true Queen come in. She took the child in her
arms, and rocked it a while, and then, shaking up its pillow, laid it
down in its cradle, and covered it over again. She did not forget
the Fawn either, but going to the corner where he was, stroked his
head, and then went silently out of the door. The nurse asked in
the morning of the guards if any one had passed into the castle
during the night; but they answered, "No, we have not seen
anybody." For many nights afterwards she came constantly, but
never spoke a word ; and the nurse saw her always, but she would
not trust herself to speak about it to any one.

When some time had passed away, the Queen one night began
to speak, and said,—

> "How fares my child? how fares my fawn?
> Twice more will I come, but never again."

The nurse made no reply; but, when she had disappeared, went to
the King, and told him all. The King exclaimed, "Oh, mercy!
what does this mean?—the next night I will watch myself by the

child." So in the evening he went into the nursery, and about
midnight the Queen appeared, and said,—

"How fares my child? how fares my fawn?
Once more will I come, but never again."

And she nursed the child, as she usually did, and then disappeared.
The King dared not speak; but he watched the following night, and
this time she said—

"How fares my child? how fares my fawn?
This time have I come, but never again."

At these words the King could
hold back no longer, but, springing
up, cried, "You can be no other
than my dear wife!" Then she
answered, "Yes, I am your dear
wife;" and at that moment her life
was restored by God's mercy, and
she was again as beautiful and
charming as ever. She told the
King the fraud which the witch
and her daughter had practised
upon him, and he had them both
tried, and sentence was pronounced
against them. The little Fawn
was disenchanted, and received
once more
his human
form; and
the Brother
and Sister
lived hap-
pily to-
gether to
the end of
their days.

M·L·A

DUMMLING AND
THE THREE FEATHERS

ONCE upon a time there lived a King who had three sons; the two elder were learned and bright, but the youngest said very little and appeared somewhat foolish, so he was always known as Dummling.

When the King grew old and feeble, feeling that he was nearing his end, he wished to leave the crown to one of his three sons, but could not decide to which. He thereupon settled that they should travel, and that the one who could obtain the most splendid carpet should ascend the throne when he died.

So that there could be no disagreement as to the way each one should go, the King conducted them to the courtyard of the Palace, and there blew three feathers, by turn, into the air, telling his sons to follow the course that the three feathers took.

Then one of the feathers flew eastwards, another westwards, but the third went straight up towards the sky, though it only sped a short distance before falling to earth.

Therefore one son travelled towards the east, and the second went to the west, both making fun of poor Dummling who was obliged to stay where his feather had fallen. Then Dummling, sitting down and feeling rather miserable after his brothers had gone, looked about him, and noticed that near to where his feather lay was a trap-door. On lifting this up he perceived a flight of steps down which he went. At the bottom was another door, so he knocked upon it, and then heard a voice calling:

> " Maiden, fairest, come to me,
> Make haste to ope the door,
> A mortal surely you will see,
> From the world above is he,
> We'll help him from our store."

And then the door was flung open, and the young man found himself facing a big toad sitting in the centre of a number of young toads. The big toad addressed him, asking him what he wanted.

Dummling, though rather surprised when he saw the toads, and heard them question him, being good-hearted replied politely:

"I am desirous to obtain the most splendid carpet in the world; just now it would be extremely useful to me."

The toad who had just spoken, called to a young toad, saying:

> " Maiden, fairest, come to me,
> 'Tis a mortal here you see;
> Let us speed all his desires,
> Giving him what he requires."

Immediately the young toad fetched a large box. This the old one opened, and took out an exquisite carpet, of so beautiful a design, that it certainly could have been manufactured nowhere upon the earth.

Taking it with grateful thanks, Dummling went up the flight of steps, and was once more in the Palace courtyard.

The two elder brothers, being of the opinion that the youngest was so foolish that he was of no account whatever in trying to obtain the throne, for they did not think he would find anything at all, had said to each other:

"It is not necessary for us to trouble much in looking for the carpet!" so they took from the shoulders of the first peasant they came across a coarse shawl, and this they carried to their father.

At the same time Dummling appeared with his beautiful carpet, which he presented to the King, who was very much surprised, and said:

"By rights the throne should be for my youngest son."

But when the two brothers heard this, they gave the old King no rest, saying:

"How is it possible that Dummling, who is not at all wise, could control the affairs of an important kingdom. Make some other condition, we beg of you!"

"Well," agreed the father, "the one who brings me the most magnificent ring shall succeed to my throne," and once more he took his sons outside the Palace. Then, again, he blew three feathers into the air to show the direction each one should go; whereupon the two elder sons' went east and west, but Dummling's flew straight up, and fell close by the trap-door.

Then the youngest son descended the steps as before, and upon seeing the large toad he talked with her, and told her what he desired.

So the big box was brought, and out of it the toad

handed him a ring which was of so exquisite a workmanship that no goldsmith's could equal it.

Meanwhile the two elder brothers made fun of the idea of Dummling searching for a ring, and they decided to take no needless trouble themselves.

Therefore, finding an old iron ring belonging to some harness, they took that to the King.

Dummling was there before them with his valuable ring, and immediately upon his showing it, the father declared that in justice the kingdom should be his.

In spite of this, however, the two elder sons worried the poor King into appointing one test further, before bestowing his kingdom, and the King, giving way, announced that the one who brought home the most beautiful woman should inherit the crown.

Then Dummling again descended to the large toad, and made known to her that he wished to find the most beautiful woman alive.

" The most beautiful woman is not always at hand," said the toad, "however, you shall have her."

Then she gave to him a scooped-out turnip to which half a dozen little mice were attached. The young man regarded this a trifle despondently, for it had no great resemblance to what he was seeking.

" What can I make of this ? " he asked.

" Only place in it one of my young toads," replied the large toad, " and then you can decide how to use it."

From the young toads around the old toad, the young man seized one at hazard, and placed it in the scooped-out turnip, but hardly was it there when the most astounding change occurred, for the toad was transformed into a wondrously lovely maiden, the turnip became an elegant carriage, and the six mice were turned into handsome horses. The young man kissed the maiden and drove off to bring her to the King.

Not long afterwards the two brothers arrived.

In the same way, as the twice before, they had taken no trouble about the matter, but had picked up the first passable looking peasant woman whom they had happened to meet.

After glancing at the three, the King said: " Without doubt, at my death the kingdom will be Dummling's."

Once more the brothers loudly expressed their discontent, and gave the King no peace, declaring :

" It is impossible for us to agree to Dummling becoming ruler of the kingdom," and they insisted that the women should be required to spring through a hoop which was suspended from the ceiling in the centre of the hall, thinking to themselves, " Now, certainly our peasants will get the best of it, they are active and sturdy, but that fragile lady will kill herself if she jumps."

To this, again, the King consented, and the peasants were first given trial.

They sprang through the hoop, indeed, but so clumsily that they fell, breaking their arms and legs.

Upon which the lovely lady whom Dummling had brought home, leapt through as lightly as a fawn, and this put an end to all contention.

So the crown came to Dummling, who lived long, and ruled his people temperately and justly.

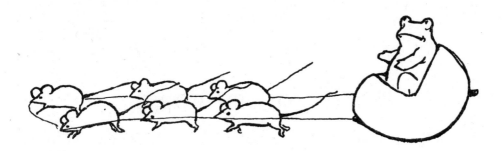

THE GOLDEN GOOSE

THERE was once a man who had three sons. The youngest was called Dummerly, and was on all occasions scorned and ill-treated by the whole family. It happened that the eldest took it into his head one day to go into the forest to cut wood; and his mother gave him a delicious meat pie and a bottle of wine to take with him, that he might sustain himself at his work. As he went into the forest, a little old man bid him good day, and said, " Give me a little bit of meat from your plate, and a little wine out of your flask; I am very hungry and thirsty." But this clever young man said, "Give you my meat and wine! No, I thank you; there would not be enough left for me;" and he went on his way. He soon began to chop down a tree; but he had not worked long before he missed his stroke, and cut himself, and was obliged to go home to have the wound bound up. Now, it was the little old man who caused him this mischief.

Next the second son went out to work; and his mother gave him, too, a meat pie and a bottle of wine. And the same little old man encountered him also, and begged him for something to eat and drink. But he, too, thought himself extremely clever, and said, "Whatever you get, I shall be without; so go your way!" The little man made sure that he should have his reward; and the second stroke that he struck at a tree, hit him on the leg, so that he too was compelled to go home.

Then Dummerly said, "Father, I should like to go and cut fuel too." But his father replied, "your brothers have both maimed themselves; you had better stop at home, for you know nothing of the job." But Dummerly was very urgent; and at last his father said, "Go your way; you will be wiser when you have suffered for your foolishness." And his mother gave him only some dry bread, and a bottle of sour ale; but when he went into the forest, he met the little old man, who said, "Give me some meat and drink, for I am very hungry and thirsty." Dummerly said, "I have nothing but dry bread and sour beer; if that will do for you, we will sit down and eat it together." So they sat down, and when the lad took out his bread, behold it was turned into a splendid meat pie, and his sour beer became delicious wine! They ate and drank heartily; and when they had finished, the little man said, "As you have a kind heart, and have been willing to share everything with me, I will bring good to you. There stands an old tree; chop it down, and you will find something at the root." Then he took his leave, and went his way.

Dummerly set to work, and cut down the tree; and when it fell, he discovered in a hollow under the roots a goose with plumage

of pure gold. He took it up, and went on to an inn, where he proposed to sleep for the night. The landlord had three daughters; and when they saw the goose, they were very curious to find out what this wonderful bird could be, and wished very much to pluck one of the feathers out of its tail. At last the eldest said, "I must and will have a feather." So she waited till his back was turned, and then caught hold of the goose by the wing; but to her great surprise, there she stuck, for neither hand nor finger could she pull away again. Presently in came the second sister, and thought to have a feather too; but the instant she touched her sister, there she too hung fast.   At last came the third, and desired a feather; but the other two cried out, "Keep away! for heaven's sake, keep away!"   However she did not understand what they meant.   "If they are there," thought she, "I may as well be there too," so she went up to them.   But the moment she touched her sisters she stuck fast, and hung to the goose as they did.   And so they abode with the goose all night.

The next morning Dummerly carried off the goose under his arm, and took no heed of the three girls, but went out with them sticking fast behind; and wherever he journeyed, the three were obliged to follow, whether they wished or not, as fast as their legs could carry them.

In the middle of a field the parson met them; and when he saw the procession, he said, "Are you not ashamed of yourselves, you bold girls, to run after the young man like that over the fields? Is that proper behaviour?"

Then he took the youngest by the hand to lead her away; but the moment he touched her he, too, hung fast, and followed in the procession.

Presently up came the clerk; and when he saw his master, the parson, running after the three girls, he was greatly surprised, and said, "Hollo! hollo! your reverence! whither so fast! There is a christening to-day."

Then he ran up, and caught him by the gown, and instantly he was fast too.

As the five were thus trudging along, one after another, they met two labourers with their mattocks coming from work; and the parson called out to them to set him free.   But hardly had they touched him, when they, too, joined the ranks, and so made seven, all running after Dummerly and his goose.

At last they came to a city, where reigned a King who had an only daughter.   The princess was of so thoughtful and serious a turn of mind that no one could make her laugh; and the King had announced to all the world that whoever could make her laugh should have her for his wife.   When the young man heard this, he went to her with the goose and all its followers; and as soon as she saw the seven all hanging together, and running about, treading on each other's heels, she could not help bursting into a long and loud laugh.

Then Dummerly claimed her for his bride; the wedding took place, and he was heir to the kingdom, and lived long and happily with his wife.

M LA

THE NOSE

HAVE you ever heard the story of the three poor soldiers, who, after having fought hard in the wars, set out on their homeward road begging their way as they went?

They had travelled a long distance, sick at heart with their ill-fortune at thus being turned loose on the world in their old days, when one evening they came to a deep, gloomy wood through which they had to pass. Night came quickly upon them, and they found themselves obliged, however unwillingly, to sleep in the wood; so to make all as safe as possible, it was agreed that two should lie down and sleep, while the third sat up and watched lest wild beasts should break in and tear them to pieces; when he was tired he was to wake one of the others and sleep in his turn, and so on with the third, so sharing the work fairly among them.

The two who were to rest first, soon lay down and fell fast asleep, and the other made himself a good fire beneath the trees and sat down beside it to keep watch. He had not sat long when, quite suddenly, up came a little man in a red jacket. "Who's there?" said he. "A friend," answered the soldier. "What sort of a friend?" "An old broken soldier," said the other, "with his two comrades who have nothing left to live on; come, sit down and warm yourself." "Well, my good fellow," said the little man, "I will do what I can for you; take this and show it to your comrades in the morning." Then he took out an old cloak and gave it to the soldier, telling him that whenever he put it over his shoulders anything that he wished for would be granted; then the little man made him a bow and walked away.

The second soldier's time to watch soon came, and the first lay down to sleep; but the second man had not sat by himself long, before up came the little man in the red jacket again. The soldier treated him in a friendly way, as his comrade had done, and the little man gave him a purse, which he told him was always full of gold, let him take out as much as he would.

Then the third soldier's turn to watch came, and he also received a visit from the little man, who gave him a wonderful horn that drew crowds around it whenever it was played, and made every one forget his business to come and dance to its sweet music.

In the morning each told his story and showed his treasure; and as they all were fond of one another and were old friends, they agreed to travel together to see the world, and for a time only to make use of the wonderful purse. And thus they spent their days very merrily, till at last they began to weary of this roving life, and thought they would like to have a home of their own. So the first soldier put on his cloak, and wished for a fine castle. Instantly it stood before their eyes; large gardens and green lawns spread around it, and flocks of sheep and goats, and herds of cattle were grazing about, and out of the gate came a splendid coach with three dapple greys to meet them and bring them home.

All this was very well for a while; but it would not do to remain at home always, so they got together all their rich clothes and servants, and ordered their coach with three horses, and set out to see a neighbouring king. Now this king had an only daughter, and as he imagined the three soldiers were kings' sons, he gave them a kind welcome. One day, as the second soldier was walking with the princess, she noticed the wonderful purse in his hand: and having asked him what it was, he was silly enough to tell her, though indeed it did not much matter, for she was a witch and knew all the marvellous things that the three soldiers brought. Now this princess was very wily and artful; so she set to work and made a purse so much like the soldier's that no one would know one from the other, and then asked him to come and see her, and made him drink some wine that she had prepared for him, till he fell fast asleep. Then she felt in his pocket, and took away the wonderful purse and in its place left the one she had made.

The next morning the soldiers set out for home, and soon after they reached their castle, happening to need some money, they went to their purse for it, and found something indeed in it, but to their great grief when they had emptied it, nothing came in the place of what they took. Then the cheat was soon found out; for the second soldier knew where he had been, and how he had told the story to the princess, and he guessed that she had cheated him. "Alas!" cried he, "poor wretches that we are, what shall we do?" "Oh!" said the first soldier, "grow no grey hairs for this mishap. I will soon get the purse back," so throwing his cloak over his shoulders, he wished himself in the princess's chamber. There he found her sitting alone, counting the gold that fell around her in a shower from the purse. But the soldier stood looking at her too long, for the moment she saw him she jumped up and cried out with all her might, "Thieves!" so that the whole court came running in and tried to seize the poor soldier, who now began to be dreadfully frightened in his turn, and thought it was high time to make the best of his way off; so, without thinking of the way of travelling that his cloak gave him, he ran to the window, opened it, and sprang out; and unluckily in his haste his cloak caught, and was left hanging, to the great delight of the princess, who knew its worth.

The poor soldier made the best of his way home to his comrades, on foot, feeling very much downcast; but the third soldier told him to cheer up, and he took his horn and blew a merry tune. At the first blast an innumerable troop of foot and horse soldiers came rushing to their aid, and they set out to make war against their enemy. Then the king's palace was besieged, and he was told that he must give up the purse and cloak, or that not one stone should be left upon another. And the king went into his daughter's chamber and talked with her; but she said, "Let me try first if I cannot get over them some other way." So she thought of a cunning plan to overreach them, and clad herself as a poor girl, with a basket on her arm, and set out by night with her maid, and went into the enemy's camp as if she wished to sell trinkets.

In the morning she began to roam about, singing songs so beautifully that all the tents were left empty, and the soldiers ran around in crowds and thought of nothing but hearing her sing. With the rest came the soldier to whom the horn belonged, and as soon as she saw him she signed to her maid, who slipped slily through the crowd and went into his tent where it was hanging, and stole it away. This being done, they both got safely back to the palace; the besieging army went away, the three wonderful presents were all left with the princess, and the three soldiers were as penniless and forlorn as when the little man with the red jacket had found them in the wood.

Poor fellows! they began to think what they should now do. " Comrades," at last said the second soldier, who had had the purse, " we had better separate. We cannot live together; let each seek his bread as best he may." So he turned to the right, and the other two to the left; for they said they would rather travel together. Then the one wandered on till he came to a wood (now this was the same wood where they had met with so much good fortune before;) and he walked on a long while till evening began to fall, when he sat down, weary, beneath a tree, and soon fell asleep.

Morning dawned, and he was greatly pleased, on opening his eyes, to see that the tree was laden with the most splendid apples. He was hungry enough, so he soon picked and ate first one, then a second, then a third apple. A strange feeling came over his nose. As he was putting the apple to his mouth something was in the way; he felt it; it was his nose, that grew and grew till it was hanging down to his breast. It did not stop there; still it grew and grew. " When will it have done growing?" he thought. And well might he ask, for by this time it reached the ground as he sat on the grass, and thus it kept creeping on till he could not bear its weight, or raise himself up; and it seemed as if it would never come to an end, for already it spread its enormous length all through the wood.

Meanwhile his comrades were journeying on, till suddenly one of them stumbled over something. "What can that be?" said the other. They looked, and could think of nothing that it was like but a nose. "We will follow it, however, and find to whom it belongs," said they; so they traced it up till at last they discovered their poor comrade lying stretched along under the apple-tree. What was to be done? They tried to carry him, but in vain. They caught an ass that was passing by, and lifted him upon its back; but it was soon tired of carrying such a load. So they sat down in despair, when up came the little man in the red jacket. "Why, how now, friend?" said he, laughing; "well, I must find a cure for you, I see." So he told them to gather a pear from a tree that grew near by, and the nose would come right again. No time was lost, and the nose was soon brought to its correct size, to the poor soldier's delight.

"I will do something more for you still," said the little man. "Take some of those pears and apples with you: whoever eats one of the apples will have his nose grow as yours did just now; but if you give him a pear, all will come right again. Go to the princess and get her to eat some of your apples; her nose will grow twenty times as long as yours did; then be smart and you will get what you want from her."

Then they thanked their old friend very gratefully for all his

kindness, and it was decided that the poor soldier who had already experienced the power of the apple should undertake the task. So he dressed himself up as a country boy, and went to the king's palace, and said he had apples to sell, such as had never been seen there before. Everyone that saw them was delighted and wished to taste, but he said they were only for the princess; and she quickly sent her maid to buy his stock. They were so ripe and red that she soon began eating, and had already finished three when she, too, began to wonder what was the matter with her nose, for it grew and grew, down to the floor, out of the window, and over the garden, to no one knew where.

Then the king proclaimed to all his kingdom, that whoever would heal her of this dreadful disease should be richly rewarded. Many tried, but the princess obtained no relief. And now the old soldier dressed himself up very stylishly as a doctor who said he could cure her; so he chopped up some of the apple, and to punish her a little more gave her a dose, saying he would call the next day and see her again. The morrow came, and, of course, instead of being better, the nose had been growing quickly all the night, and the poor princess was in a terrible fright. So the doctor chopped up a very little piece of the pear and gave it to her, and said he was sure that would do good, and he would call again the next day. Next day came, and the nose was certainly a little smaller, but yet it was longer than it was when the doctor first began to tend it.

Then he thought to himself, "I must frighten this wily princess a little more before I shall get what I want of her;" so he gave her another dose of the apple, and said he would call on the morrow. The next day came, and the nose was ten times as bad as before. "My good lady," said the doctor, "something is working against my medicine, and is too strong for it; but I know by the means of my art what it is. You have stolen goods about you, I am sure, and if you do not give them back, I can do nothing for you." But the princess denied very decidedly that she had anything of the kind. "Very well," said the doctor, "you may do as you like, but I am sure I am right, and you will die if you do not acknowledge it." Then he went to the king, and informed him how the matter stood. "Daughter," said he, "return the cloak, the purse, and the horn that you stole from the rightful owners."

Then she ordered her maid to fetch all three, and handed them to the doctor, and entreated him to give them back to the soldiers; and directly he had them, safe, he gave her a whole pear to eat, and the nose came right. And as for the doctor, he put on the cloak, wished the king and all his court a good day, and was soon with his two comrades, who lived from that time happily at home in their palace, except when they went for airings in their coach with the three dapple greys.

THE FAIRY FOLK

The Elves and the Shoemaker

ONCE upon a time there was a shoemaker who worked very hard and was extremely honest, but still he could not earn enough to live upon, and at length all he had in the world was gone, except just leather sufficient to make one pair of shoes. Then he cut them all ready to make up the next day, intending to get up early in the morning to work. His conscience was clear and his heart light amidst all his troubles; so he went quietly to bed, left all his troubles to heaven, and fell asleep. In the morning, after he had said his prayers, he sat down to his work, when, to his great astonishment, there stood the shoes, all ready made, upon the table. The good man did not know what to say or think of this strange occurrence. He looked at the workmanship; there was not one bad stitch in the whole job; all was so neat and true that it was a complete masterpiece.

That same day a customer came in, and the shoes pleased him so well that he, with pleasure, paid a price higher than usual for them; and the poor shoemaker with the money bought leather sufficient to make two pairs more. In the evening he cut out the work, and went to bed in good time that he might rise early and begin betimes next day; but he was saved all the trouble, for when he got up in the morning the work was completed ready to his hand. Presently in came buyers, who paid him well for his goods, so that he bought leather enough for four pairs more. Again he cut out the work over night, and found it finished in the morning as before; and so it went on for some time; what was prepared in the evening was always finished by daybreak, and the good man soon became thriving and prosperous again.

One evening about Christmas-time, as he and his wife were sitting over the fire talking together, he said to her, "I should like to sit up and watch to-night, that we may see who it is that comes and does my work for me." The wife liked the idea; so they left a light burning, and hid themselves in the corner of the room behind a curtain that was hung up there, and waited for what should happen.

As soon as it was midnight, there came two little naked dwarfs; and they sat themselves upon the shoemaker's bench, took up all the work that was cut out, and began to ply with their little fingers, stitching and rapping and tapping away so quickly that the shoemaker was all wonderment, and could not take his eyes off for a moment. And on they went till the job was completed, and the shoes stood ready for use upon the table. This was long before dawn; and then they scurried away as quick as lightning.

The following day the wife said to the shoemaker, "These little wights have made us rich, and we should be thankful to them, and do them a kindness in return. I am quite worried to see them run about as they do; they have nothing upon their backs to keep off the cold. I know what—I will make each of them a shirt, and a coat and vest, and a pair of breeches into the bargain; and you make each of them a little pair of shoes."

The idea pleased the good shoemaker very much; and one evening, when all the things were ready, they put them on the table in place of the work that they used to cut out, and then went and hid themselves to see what the little elves would do. About midnight they came in, and were preparing to sit down to their work as usual; but when they saw the clothes placed for them, they laughed and were highly delighted. Then they dressed themselves in the twinkling of an eye, and sprang and capered and danced about as merry as could be, till at last they danced out of the door across the green; and the shoemaker saw them no more; but all things went well with him from that time forth, as long as he lived.

THREE DAYS WITH
THE FAIRIES

ONCE upon a time there lived a poor maid-servant, who was hard-working and clean. Every day she swept the house, and put out the dust upon a high heap in front of the door.

One morning as she was about to go on with her work in the usual way, she discovered a letter on the dust-heap; she could not read it, however, so, placing her broom in a corner, she carried the letter to her master.

It was an invitation from the fairies, they requested the girl to be godmother to one of their children.

The maid could not decide what to do, but after considerable persuasion, because she was told that she would give great offence if she refused, at last she consented.

On the appointed day, three fairies came to fetch her, and they led her to a steep mountain, which the little people inhabited. This mountain was hollow, and all the things it contained were tiny, but so costly and practically made, that it is almost impossible to describe them.

The baby was lying in an ebony bed, decorated with pearls, the quilt was covered with gold embroidery, the cradle was carved out of ivory, and every article to be used for the child was made of gold.

When the maid had performed the purpose for which she had come, she desired to go back, but the fairies begged her so earnestly to stay with them three days that she agreed to their request.

Therefore she remained, and the fairy folk were so kind to her, that the time passed pleasantly and enjoyably, and on going away her pockets were filled with gold by the little people who led her out of the mountain.

As soon as the servant arrived at home, and found the broom standing where she had left it, she took it up, and began to sweep, ready to do her accustomed work.

Upon which some strangers came out of the house, and enquired who she was, and what she was doing.

The girl had imagined it was only three days that she had been staying with the fairy folk, but it was really three years, and her old master and mistress had passed away.

THE CHANGELING

THE fairies carried off a child from the cradle, and in its place the mother found a changeling with huge head and staring eyes, that did nothing but eat and drink.

In her grief at having such a creature instead of her own bright, bonny baby, the woman went to ask a neighbour's advice. This neighbour was a wise person, and she told the mother that she must take the changeling and place it on the kitchen hearth, after that she should light the fire, and then boil some water in two egg-shells.

At this the changeling would be obliged to laugh, and when once it laughed the fairies' power was over.

Then the mother did all, just as the neighbour advised, and when she put the egg-shells, with the water in them, over the kitchen fire, the fairy-child exclaimed :

"I am as old, it's plain,
    As your age once again.
    But never have I heard tell
    Of cooking in an egg-shell."

Then the changeling chuckled right merrily, and, as soon as
it laughed, appeared a procession of little people, carrying the right
child, which they laid upon the hearth, and then went off taking
the fairy-child with them.

THIS BOOK BELONGS TO

Deirdre Simmon

Grimm's Fairy Tales £1.25
retold by Amabel Williams-Ellis

This is a collection of some of the most famous Grimm
stories such as Snow White and the Seven Dwarfs, the Goose
Girl, The Wolf and the Seven Little Kids, Mrs Owl, and
many others, all brought up to date and beautifully told and
illustrated.

Hans Andersen's Fairy Tales £1.25
Books I and II

Two volumes of Hans Andersen's Fairy Tales, with beautiful colour plates and line drawings of W Heath Robinson's illustrations. Here is The Snow Queen, The Ugly Duckling, The Nightingale, The Red Shoes, The Wild Swans and so many of the other stories that you may have heard of.

You can buy these and other Piccolo books from booksellers and newsagents; or direct from the following address:
Pan Books, Cavaye Place, London SW10 9PG
Send purchase price plus 15p for the first book and 5p for each additional book, to allow for postage and packing
Price applicable in UK
While every effort is made to keep prices low, it is sometimes necessary to increase prices at short notice. Pan Books reserve the right to show on covers new retail prices which may differ from those advertised in the text or elsewhere